good deed rain

"I'm sure you've thought about there being other worlds than this." He shut his eyes again for a moment. Could he smell that rich air? Yes, just for a second before it was overcome by this room. "It's true. You just went to one. You were lucky, most people only imagine them." Before they could speak, he had to know, "Did you find any flowers?"

THE WALLPAPER WORLD

The WALLPAPER WORLD © 2025
Allen Frost, Good Deed Rain
Bellingham, Washington
ISBN 978-1-0882-5064-8

Writing & Drawings: Allen Frost
Cover Design: Robert Millis
Quotes:
Yoko Ono, *Grapefruit*, Simon & Schuster, NY, 1964
& from *The Mike Douglas Show*, February 14, 1972
Apple: TFK!

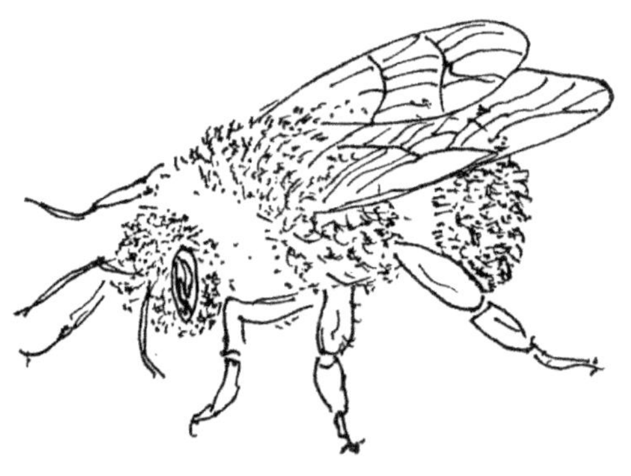

"A dream you dream alone may be a dream, but a dream two people dream together is a reality."
        —Yoko Ono

THE WALLPAPER WORLD

Allen Frost

Good Deed Rain ◊ Bellingham, Washington ◊ 2025

INTRODUCTION

Well, it's the last day of June and I'm about to mow the lawn. This isn't quite the job you might think. I still use a push-mower relic from the days of Buddy Holly. It must weigh a good eighty pounds, it's like shoving a stalled Packard on a dirt road. Secondly there are the flowers: clover, buttercups, daisies and dandelions which I do my best to avoid. The patches of them will remain like a crocheted blanket. Then there are the animals. Our dog sees this chore as a game, she drops sticks and balls in front of the blades and tackles my legs as I walk. Also this is rabbit time, a couple babies and their mother live in the yard. I'm careful not to disturb the padded down tunnels they use. I leave them some prized sorrel and what looks like a patch of lush watercress. By the end of it all, it looks like I've hardly been here, pushing the jukebox back to the barn, leaving what a breeze might have done, stamping the lawn like wallpaper.

CHAPTERS

1
OSAKA

The Daily ran an ad in the classifieds:

**ARE YOU HAPPY
WHERE YOU ARE?**

That was followed by his name, Lloyd Clatter, and his telephone number. It took longer than he thought to find someone. It turned out most of his replies were from people who said they were *not* happy here, they wanted to go somewhere else. That wasn't the answer he wanted. As if they expected him to send them away. If they wanted that, they could take a rocket to the moon or the far-flung colonies.

The ad ran for three weeks until two people answered correctly. They were best friends. They sounded perfect. He was going to How Now? to meet them.

The café was a half-hour walk. Bird songs were leaking through the sounds of the city.

Lloyd didn't have a problem with where he was. He liked the neighborhood even when it was raining. He loved the seasons and the ever-changing weather. Winter was nearly over—this was one of those days you knew that was true. Sun shined on the bare maple branches parked along the curb. Pretty soon green leaves would wake up. Across the street a seagull stood on the roof of Garden apartments and watched everyone. Lloyd turned at the corner and above the traffic the park was visible a block away.

As soon as he crossed Pacific Avenue, a squirrel showed him where to go, under an archway, this is the park where I live, hopping off the path and climbing up a tree. Shrubs were budding. Small white flowers lined the path. He took a deep breath. A sound he hadn't heard in months, leaves in the breeze. The smell of the earth and new growth. The smell of spring, he could take a bite of it, he could live on flowers. He imagined a world like this. A sign pointed to another path, Osaka. His heels pressed into the gravel and left a trail of half circles. He joined more footprints, a lot of people visited this part of the park at this time. It was snowing. The cherry trees circled the pond and snowed along the creek. A steep halfmoon wooden bridge arched over the water. A pagoda temple was the background for cameras. Lloyd walked slowly through Osaka. He had plenty of time, the café was only a few minutes away, on Brooklyn Avenue.

He left the park on the Sunnyside Avenue side. Houses facing the park waited for spring to hurry up and pull summer along so doors could stay open, and the windows could let a breeze in. It wouldn't take long. This was the first warm day in a while, it was visiting them like a fox, warily testing the alleys and backyards. It was okay, it was a beautiful day, spring was on the way.

The café was getting near. He turned onto Brooklyn.

Lloyd loved this world, but he knew where there was another one.

RADIO
CASETTE PLAYER
WM-FX30
◁ AUTO REVERSE ▷
WALKMAN FM/AM
FM
AM

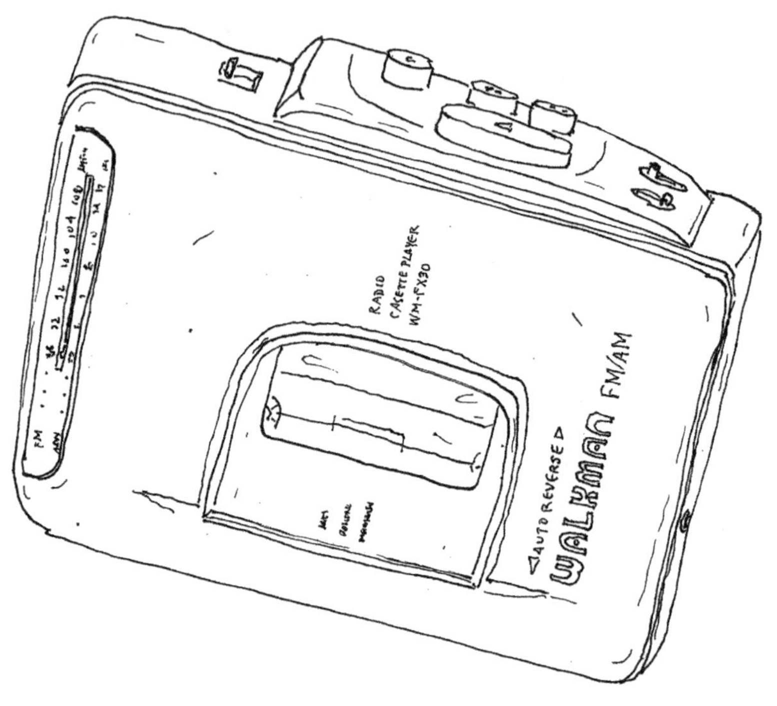

not far away

2
BROOKLYN AVENUE

Lloyd read his notes and was pleased. Pete and Natalia were the perfect astronauts. Astronauts? No, that wasn't quite correct, they didn't need rockets. As far as they knew they weren't going to another planet.

Were they though?

Not far away in his apartment, the sun was shining through the window making a square of light on the wall. It seemed so peaceful.

What was really on the other side of the wallpaper?

Lloyd didn't tell them yet.

Brooklyn Avenue would seem like a dream.

A girl started to play guitar on the little stage in the corner. Her voice began to sing like a flower. It bloomed at the far end of the room. Lloyd poured the last of his tea into his cup. Not much. He thought about ordering another teapot. Or maybe it was time to go. He made some money appear in his hand, some dollars and a silver coin from Ireland. The harp on it shined.

What was that song?

Past the tables, the dishwasher lugging a rattling tub, he saw the girl with the guitar was Natalia. His notes didn't include she was a musician. Would that matter? Would she make songs of the other world and would people believe they were true? That shouldn't matter, people did that all the time. It was a part of art.

When her hands stopped and the song was done, it sat in the space of air the way smoke will before it disappears. Someone up front clapped politely. That was Pete. They surprised Lloyd. He thought they were gone but they stayed around. How Now? was the sort of café where you could stay all day.

Lloyd stood up. He gathered his empty teapot and cup and walked towards the dishwasher crossing the room with a new dish tub. Lloyd met him as he set it down. Lloyd's cup was all alone for now.

Natalia was putting her guitar in its case. Pete stood next to her saying something. They were in the middle of words when Lloyd reached them.

"I like your song," he told her.

"Peter wrote it."

"Really? Amazing. I didn't know you two had such hidden talents."

They laughed. They were fifteen. They were the happiest of all the people Lloyd had seen.

"We thought about your job," said Natalia. "We thought about it and decided we want to."

"That's great. I think you're both perfect. You're hired!"

"When does it start?" Pete asked.

"Oh, well, whenever you have time."

Natalia and Pete looked at each other a moment. "Why not now? It's Saturday, we're just wandering around."

"Seeing the sights," Pete added.

"Okay then. What are we waiting for? Let's go!"

3
WHAT TO KNOW ABOUT CROWS

Natalia pointed at the crow watching them and told the story about her father. He started feeding the crows as he walked to work every morning. First with bread, then he found their favorite was cat food. He would scatter a little meal and carry on, looking over his shoulder to see them land. They would fly down from housetops, trees and telephone poles. They kept eyes on the city and they watched for him. He was part of their days. He thought of them as friends.

Natalia stopped talking when they reached the streetcorner and she pressed the silver button on the traffic pole. They were waiting for the crosswalk light.

"Then he saw a crow steal a baby robin from a nest. Dad scared the crow away, but it was too late. After that, the crows decided he wasn't one of them. He couldn't be trusted. They crossed him off their list."

"He should bake them a cake," Pete said. That would work for Pete. He loved cake.

"Maybe. What do you think, Mr. Clatter?"

Cars stopped for the red light. They started across.

Lloyd chanted, "Four and twenty blackbirds baked in a pie. Their only concern is survival. It reminds me of an old nursery rhyme." They reached the other side of the street. "And those fairytales full of rules and lessons, wrong and right, where you learn the consequences of your actions, usually the hard way. There are forces at play. Actually—that's something you'll have to be aware of when you go into the test room. Be aware. Stick to the plan and there won't be any trouble." That wasn't quite true.

Pete pointed to their right. "Are we going on campus?" The university was two streets away. When he saw the ad in the college paper, he figured it was another one of those campus jobs. He knew a boy at school who cleaned rabbit cages. When he read the ad to her, Pete was happy, Natalia was too.

Lloyd said, "No, we're going to the Clover. We don't need a laboratory, this isn't that sort of job." He felt they were right to be curious, most people would be, but they were different, he knew they weren't worried about anything bad. Besides, they had each other. "It ought to be easy for you, all you need to do is bring something back."

"That seems pretty simple," Natalia said.

"Unless it's an elephant!" Pete didn't mind that thought. It would be fun to lead an elephant.

Lloyd laughed. "It's not an elephant."

Pete was glad. That solved the problem of getting an elephant out an apartment door. Or down an elevator.

Lloyd stopped next to a break in the cement where weeds grew. "That's what you want to look for."

"Dandelions?"

"Dandelions in a room?"

Lloyd nodded. He wondered what they were picturing. They would find out. Clover Apartments was standing there in the middle of other buildings, waiting, hands in pockets, windows like buttons running up and down.

4
AROUND THE CLOVER

Lloyd Clatter opened the door to a one room apartment on the fifth floor. Natalia and Pete looked around, there wasn't much to it, no furniture or pictures or TV. No dishes cluttered the kitchenette, an open cupboard showed an empty shelf. The window held a blue sky.

"Is this the test room?" Pete asked. There was no sign of yellow flowers.

"No, I live here," although it looked as if he had just landed. "I'll show you where you're going." The floorboards creaked. Around them the walls were foggy colored paint except for the place in the corner where he led them, a tall door-shape of patterned wallpaper. "This is the door."

"Oh," said Natalia.

"When you open it, you'll be…I guess I need to explain, it's more than just a room."

"Oh," Natalia said again.

"A door to where?" Pete asked.

"I can't explain now, just trust me, you need to see to believe. When you're there, be real quick, get the dandelions and get back."

Natalia laughed at that, "We can be fast. Peter was on track at school."

Pete smiled. He thought about explaining, but you can't tell an inside joke.

"Okay," said Lloyd. He couldn't think of another way. "This is how it works." He turned his arms, "Lift the wallpaper edge, it will open like a door."

"We just go in, look around for dandelions and gather some," said Natalia.

"And don't forget to come back. This is where you're happiest, right?"

They told Lloyd of course. How hard could it be to get flowers and come back?

Lloyd retreated another few paces until he was in the middle of the room. He didn't want to be near the wallpaper. The world on the other side could pull him in. He closed his eyes. He had lost people in there before. He didn't tell Natalia and Pete that. The possible danger was so rare. Suddenly he was scared they would go. If they didn't return, what would he do? He would have to find them. He didn't want to. All at once he hoped he would hear them say, "Nothing's happening." Not everyone could go through wallpaper. It would work or it wouldn't.

He kept his eyes closed. The radiator clucked. He could hear the dull sigh of the city. I-5 was close, the streets around the Clover were busy breathing. When he heard the wallpaper luff flat, Lloyd opened his eyes. The kids were gone.

5

A BETTER PLACE

It was a sunny day. It always was. Two men stepped from a black truck. They were well-known comedians a hundred years ago. They got a ladder off the roof of their Model T. They didn't fumble or trip or drop it, the ladder was easy to carry through traffic to the other side of the street and set up at a steep angle against a brick wall. They had no trouble returning to the truck to get buckets of wheat paste. One carried those and the other carried a long poster roll and back they went to the ladder. They had a system that worked perfectly. No ragtime piano was playing. The thin one led the way up the ladder, up, up, up they went. Nobody opened a window to shake out a carpet, no bird jumped out from a nest on a window ledge. No butterfly made them sneeze. At the end of the climb, fifty feet in the air, one held the paper facedown and unrolled as the other swabbed the underside with glue.

The wide poster slowly covered the bricks.

Gigantic black letters formed:

W A N T E D

Below that, a portrait began to show, the top of someone's head. There was still a lot of face to unfurl.

For a moment from the ladder's height, Stan Laurel could see over the rooftops to the big grassy dandelion field. The flowers filled it with bright yellow lightbulbs. Stan kept one glowing in a pocket, everyone did, there were plenty to share. Oliver Hardy descended another step. A little water slopped from the bucket. It didn't splash onto a cat that caused the ladder to rattle and shake them off. They continued with their work.

Laurel and Hardy moved pianos up stairs, did plumbing and carpentry, flew in biplanes, met ghosts, stray dogs, jitterbugs and sailors without tangling or failure. You could count on them. They made the world a better place. When they were done with this job they carried the ladder back to their truck. Tomorrow is another movie. The traffic slowed for them and people leaned from the trolley to cheer and wave.

6
THE DANDELION THIEF

Pete and Natalia stepped from the brick wall into an alley. They went through wallpaper on the fifth floor and were now at street level. They were too surprised to say anything at first. It was warmer, like July, the air was almost heavy with sunshine. Pete stood next to Natalia like a statue. She lifted her shoe from a shallow pool of water. A horse pulling a loaded cart echoed down the alley from the avenue. Marble towers grew.

"Look at that," Pete said. The cart was filled with a mound of dandelions. A green and white trolley went by, going the other way. Its wheels clacked, the poles sparked on the wires overhead.

Pete said, "Do we run after the flowers?"

"Hold on, Peter," she pinched his shirt sleeve.

"Where are we?"

"Mr. Clatter asked us to get the dandelions and get back. We still have time to catch it."

Natalia looked to their left as the alley channeled between the two tall brick buildings to another street. A distant trolley. A herd of orange and blue zebras. They were in the downtown of a big city.

Pete smiled, "That's funny you told him I was in track."

"Well, you were! And you broke the world record, right? I didn't tell him that." She loved that story. It was part of his mythology. Her eyes got bright when she replayed it. Then when she turned around, her hand gripped Peter's arm.

She stared above their door in the wall. The bricks were still damp, seeping from the poster that was glued on.

"It's Mr. Clatter," Pete said.

Natalia read aloud, "Wanted. Lloyd Clatter. Thief and General Nuisance."

"Uh oh..."

Natalia said, "I think we better get back. I think we better ask about that."

"Yeah, but..." Pete was thinking about the dandelions. He reminded her that's what they were here for. The avenue had carts piled high, they could see if another was coming. Grab a handful and run back to the door.

"I don't know, Peter. Maybe we're not allowed to. What if taking flowers is a crime? Maybe that's why he's a thief. Maybe that's why he sent us."

"Oh, Nat, I think we're okay. They're not driving them in armored cars. We—" his words trailed off as he spotted something on the cobblestones. A crumpled yellow flower. Someone had tossed it down like a spent cigarette.

clickety wheels

7
A BIRD BY ACCIDENT

Lloyd Clatter was waiting for them. Not that he really noticed their absence, only a couple seconds passed since they vanished. He was still in the same place in the middle of the room as the wallpaper opened. He quickly shut his eyes. The light from there had an effect on him, like an undertow. He couldn't resist for long. He was only a kite flying here, waiting to be pulled back to the ground. He put his hands over his ears so he wouldn't hear a bird by accident, or the clickety wheels of a trolley.

Pete shut the paper door behind them.

The Thief and General Nuisance opened his eyes and regarded them. They didn't look as happy as he hoped.

"Where were we?" said Natalia. There was a lot more she wanted to say, that was only the start.

"That's a fair question." That was always the first thing someone asked him when they returned. And Lloyd would explain there's no one reality, beside everything you see there's a shadow. "I'm sure you've thought about there being other worlds than this." He shut his eyes again for a moment. Could he smell that rich air? Yes, just for a second before it was overcome by this room. "It's true. You just went to one. You were lucky, most people only imagine them." Before they could speak, he had to know, "Did you find any flowers?"

"We found out you're a thief," Natalia said.

Lloyd slowly nodded. "Yes. When I left. I wasn't happy there anymore. I don't know why. I have no good reason. Well…I heard about this place, where you have day and night, where you have good and bad. I wanted to come here, so I did, the only way I could think of. I took their wallpaper. I guess you could call it stealing. I just wanted to experience this world. Turns out I like it here," he admitted. "But I need the flowers to survive here."

"You're also a general nuisance," Pete said.

Lloyd shrugged. "I went back a few times. I wasn't as courteous as I should have been. They

36

caught on. Now I play it safe. I find other people to get flowers for me."

"Happy people?" Natalia asked.

"Well, yes. It's beautiful there. I mean, I got tired of it, I'm from there, I saw the same sunny day over and over. But some people like that, sometimes they go through the wallpaper and decide not to come back."

"What happens if they do?"

"Then I have to get them. They can't stay there for long, they begin to weaken…the same thing happens to me being here if I don't get those dandelions."

Natalia said, "What if someone sees us taking them? I don't want to do anything wrong."

"You aren't. It's fine, they'll never miss a few flowers. You saw how many there are. Besides, flowers grow back—if a bank gets robbed, they print more money. Wait til you see the field! You will! That is, if you don't mind returning." He drooped. "I'm sorry, I'm so tired…I'm running out of steam."

That was when Pete handed him the flower. There wasn't much to it, a wilted yellow petal ball that he carried through the wallpaper.

8
JOHN AUDUBON

Across the alley, perched far up on the fire escape railing, a toucan watched them walk out of the wall. Not much had changed except for the bird being there. It turned its beak tracking them as they went. Nearing the street was like walking on the sand through the beachgrass towards the growing sound of the ocean surf. Natalia wanted to hurry to wherever the field was. Mr. Clatter said they wouldn't be far from it, he promised they couldn't miss it.

"It's a wonderful sight," he told them. If only he wasn't an outlaw, if only he could go back long enough to lay down in that world. One day he would. It would be like waking up. This America would vanish like a dream.

"Come on, let's find that field," Natalia said, two steps ahead of Pete. She wanted to run, she felt like she could skate across the cobblestones, gain speed and leap. But what was taking Peter, why couldn't he keep up?

"Hey Nat!" he called down to her.

She stopped and turned and looked towards the sky. He was floating in the height between the buildings. "Peter! What are you doing?"

"I'm flying!" he laughed. "It's easy!" He pedaled his legs and moved forwards. He held his arms outstretched and steered like a bird. "It's fun!"

She laughed too. He looked like a circus act, slowly riding an invisible bike on a tightrope at the top of a tent. He circled and waved at her. "How are you doing that, Peter?"

"I don't know, I just started to fly. Try it! See if you can."

She raised her arms.

"That's right." He was treading water in the air. "Take a step and climb like walking up stairs."

John Audubon with all his pictures of birds could have painted her flying, found on a page somewhere between Nashville Swamp-Warbler and the Nighthawk.

She wobbled a little, but soon she was steady and hovering next to him. Flying felt natural, the way so many things do in a dream. She turned like a clock hand, like a horse on a carousel.

He pointed ahead. She spun back to him so she could see. The alley continued over the backs of a trolley and carts, on to the other side of the street, leading to a place that was green in the distance. "There's the field."

They both ducked as the toucan rippled off its perch and flew that way.

9
FLYING

Another three seconds passed in Lloyd Clatter's apartment. That one little flower they brought him had done wonders. His mind was made pleasant, he felt light enough to fly. He couldn't help himself—careless as a drifting campfire ash, his feet left the floor. His thoughts were clear of worries as he ballooned to the ceiling.

This was Natalia and Pete's second time in the wallpaper world. If he had a crystal ball or some Flash Gordon invention he could have seen them. By now they probably figured out when you're in there, you have the powers of someone in a dream. You can do anything you can let yourself think of. That was the magic of traveling to another world. Lloyd had that same ability when he was here.

That was part of the appeal. He could open the window and float outside and be a miracle. Can you imagine? A man seen flying over Brooklyn Avenue…

It was a thrill he only got here in America, where an otherworldly flower had superpowers.

Without any wish to do otherwise, he found himself edging across the ceiling towards the wallpaper door. It was calling him. Aren't you ready to return? Sometimes, in the middle of the night especially, he heard the paper riffle. All will be forgiven. Just bring the door with you, come home…No. He didn't need to, not as long as the kids brought him flowers. A dandelion from where he was from could turn America into a wonderland.

If he glided down, if he unpeeled a little of the door, he could see them flying above the next alley that led to the flowers. If they flew a bit higher they would see the city was a circle, surrounded by a moat, with a field on the other side in a Saturn ring around it.

They went past windows and could see people inside rooms. A cat watched them. A girl waved at them. The toucan descended towards a balcony and landed on an orange tree. Underneath them, the alley stopped at a path that curved against the moat. They were lucky they were flying, the bridge crossing was half a mile away. It was a big city. The marble shined with sunlight. Trees grew on roofs and birds flew between them. Pete thought it would be fun to land and explore. He was about to ask Natalia.

"Is that a shark?"

It was. The fin cut the water surface. There were others too and deeper were shadowy larger things.

Pete and Natalia quickly reacted to the sight by pumping their legs and waving their arms to gain height.

Pete said, "I'm glad we didn't try to swim."

Natalia waited until they were past the water. "Me too!"

When an airplane travels for hours across the Pacific and finally finds Hawaii, you can look out the oval window and see whales. Your shadow will skim across blue waves, onto shore and lower and lower almost skimming the same jungle-green where dandelions grow by the thousands.

10
ANOTHER WAY

Lloyd Clatter should have told them more about where they were going, how that wallpaper world was like a dream they could do anything in, but that information could cause problems.

Lloyd remembered Farrell Kramp coming out of the Labor Now temp agency one morning. The poor guy had a face like a sack of lemons. Lloyd thought he was giving him a break when he offered him a job. Just get some flowers and come back. What could be simpler? Minutes went by and turned into hours. Lloyd could tell something went wrong. Wrong was an understatement. Finally, Lloyd took a step through the wallpaper and he couldn't believe what awaited. A golden statue of Farrell Kramp flared up from the avenue. Gray cars circled it on their way. Smoke hung in the air. Marble was replaced by black glass and steel. Banners with Kramp's name. Soldiers marching boots on the sidewalk. How could it happen? Everything fell under Kramp's spell. Having brought him here, it was up to Lloyd to erase the darkness that had fallen over the land. All that was a while ago. You'd think they would be grateful he dragged Kramp back through the wallpaper. Maybe they saw it differently, maybe they blamed him for that happening in the first place. They weren't wrong, there was no denying it was the work of a general nuisance.

The door remained closed on the wall. Kramp wasn't the only one to cause trouble, he was terrible, but there were others who took advantage, or worse, thought they were gods. The wrong person could cause a lot of damage. That's why it was important to find someone Lloyd could trust, someone who was happy with life where they were. To find help like Natalia and Pete was rare. He hoped they were doing okay. Every moment that passed in his apartment was an unknown time in a world on the other side of a wall. Where were they?

Their pockets were full. Natalia made suitcases appear too and stuffed them with more flowers. Peter made her laugh. He was holding a handful as big as a yellow sheep.

"I think we have enough," she said.

Pete said, "I agree."

She held a suitcase in each hand and tried to hop into the air and fly like Mary Poppins. It didn't work. She barely left the earth. She landed where she started, on her footprints. Peter wasn't flying either. And the sheep was losing flowers every time he landed. "Are we too heavy now?" she asked. Did flowers make that much of a difference? "How do we get back?"

Pete didn't know how he flew to begin with, he didn't need to think about how. It seemed they weren't meant to fly anymore, at least not with the dandelions. They weren't escaping by air. There had to be another way. He carried his bundle to the moat's edge. The water was peaceful. If they made a flower raft and lowered it in, they could cross the river. It was still as a velvet pool table. The clear water was beckoning. He watched the long bottom weeds swing lazily. If they just stepped onto a raft, they could float across. Then he remembered the sharks and the sea monster shapes and he backed away.

It was a puzzle that took both their minds to figure. If this was a dream you had the power to control, they could picture the door, just call for it and it will appear.

11
A BUNCH OF FLOWERS

Lloyd was thinking of Myrtle. Myrtle the Turtle. She sat on a chair in front of a boarded-up building, selling flowers on the parking lot corner. Bits of broken glass sparkled around her. Cars went by. She was stuffed in a winter coat, eyes half open. Lloyd crossed the street carrying his wallpaper roll. When he was running low on dandelions, he had to go out hunting. She looked like she would do. He bought a bunch of flowers and she followed him. He unrolled the wallpaper on the side of the building where nobody else could see and she stepped through. She must know about flowers. Hers were no good to him here. He returned the bouquet to one of the metal pots by her chair. The traffic rushed past. He hoped he would turn and see her. He could make the return trip in less than ten of our seconds, but he knew the terrain. After a minute, he opened the door to check on Myrtle. There she stood. One step away was as far as she got. She was a statue. A toucan could have landed on her shoulder. The wallpaper world was more than she could bear. She returned to her spot on Aurora Avenue and remembered nothing.

It was funny the dandelions in America didn't have the same effect. They grew all over town, especially at springtime and they looked so alike but something was missing. There was no spark. Lloyd dreamed up greenhouses and tried to grow the fluffy wallpaper seeds but they couldn't take root in the soil. They were creatures from another world. Lloyd kept the last of his dandelions in a lantern. When they ran out, he'd have to go back and throw himself on their mercy.

Then the wallpaper door burst open with pouring flowers. They flooded around Lloyd, over his shoes, rushing across the floorboards. There had never been a heist like this! Natalia and Pete were the dandelion Bonnie and Clyde. The door swept over more petals as it flapped closed. Natalia laughed.

12

IN THE WALLPAPER WORLD

Where there was nothing in the air a moment ago, Lloyd opened a vault hatch big enough to hold the pile of yellow flowers. While they heaved them in and swept the rest, Pete thought of feeding coal into a steam engine. He wondered if ships and trains ran on flowers in the wallpaper world. And people too—Pete remembered the way Mr. Clatter revived with that one small, crushed dandelion. It was miraculous, wasn't it?

Lloyd shut the vault and instantly the safe was lost in the air. Gone from sight. The empty room might be cluttered with invisible furniture. You could walk right through a grandfather clock and never hear it ticking. Lloyd was overjoyed. "I don't know what to say. I'm flabbergasted. Hi-ho the derry-o! You've done so wonderfully! My troubles are over. This haul is enough for years!" His words trilled over each other like a songbird. "Here, let me show you what I've been living on. This was all I had left. I was doomed." He reached into the air again and opened a cupboard that suddenly appeared against his hand. In the cupboard sat a lantern with a weak light. He showed them two glum dandelions tangled inside the glass.

"How do you keep pulling things out of midair?" Natalia asked.

"Oh, it's easy. In this world I can do anything. For example…" He waved his hand low and a Komodo dragon flopped into the room. It was a long way from a magician taking a rabbit from a hat. The kids jumped backwards and retreated towards the apartment door. Lloyd dropped his arms and waved them across the lizard and it slithered from existence like the dinosaurs.

"Or I can do this." Lloyd snapped his fingers— summoning a familiar wooden café table, a bench on either side.

"Is that from How Now?" Natalia said. "Did you steal that too?"

"Borrowed," Lloyd said. Rattled on the tabletop were three cups and a dented copper teapot. "Have a seat?"

"I guess so. But then we should go…"

"Of course, of course, you have things to do. I'm not keeping you. Besides, you'll be glad to know hardly any time has gone by. Please have some tea before you leave. I'd like to hear what you have to say."

Only a few feet away, they weren't able to see in the wallpaper world. Laurel and Hardy were up a ladder again. The same unfunny routine, lowering a new poster that read: Wanted. Natalia and Pete. Thieves and General Nuisances.

Lloyd said, "You must have noticed, you have powers like me when you're over there." He pointed at the wallpaper. "You can make dragons appear too. It's all a matter of mind control."

"It seems so real," said Natalia.

"I know. And this world seems so real to me. But I know it's not."

Pete said, "I liked flying."

Lloyd poured them more tea. "How did you find the door once you got the flowers?"

Laurel and Hardy took their ladder down. They

each took an end and walked without knocking anyone down. They crossed the avenue when it was safe. They loaded their truck again without everything falling all over the sidewalk. Ollie held an arm into traffic without slapping a bicyclist and he steered the black truck from the curb. They had another job at the roller rink.

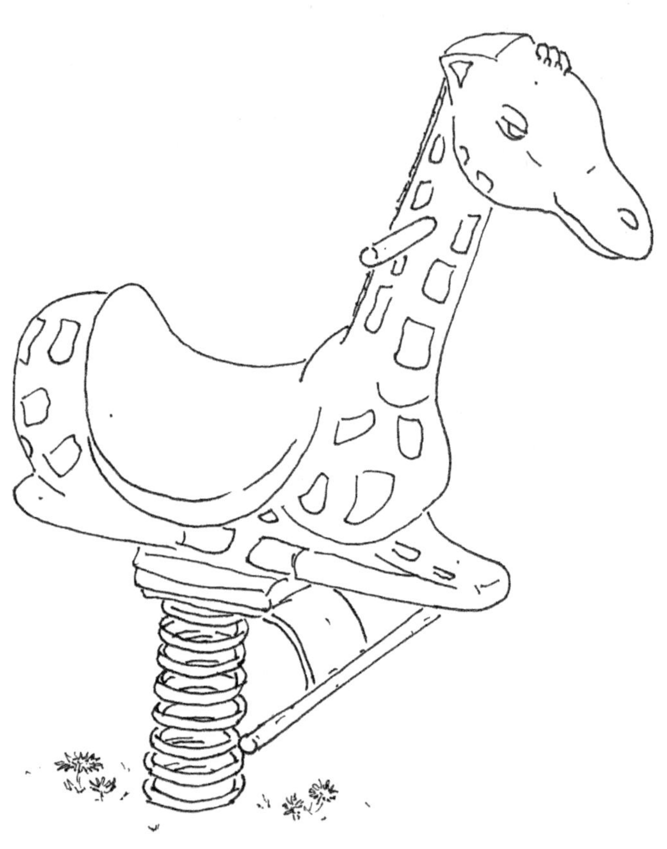

forward and back

13
DREAMLANDS

Lloyd searched for a way to explain, "You were in a dream, my dream, the same way I'm dreaming here in your world. Our dreamlands are connected by that wallpaper door."

"And you don't want to wake up," said Pete.

"The flowers we stole will keep you from waking up," Natalia said.

"I like it here. I've been here long enough it feels like home. I'll do anything to stay."

"Won't they come looking for you?"

"Sure," he laughed. "They're looking, but the history of this world goes forward and back for millions of years. I could be anywhere! For all they know I live in a shoe." Natalia had more questions, he could tell, she was the curious sort.

He felt the same way when he came to America, it was mesmerizing, he wanted to know all about it. Pete was staring into his cup. Pete already believed in other worlds. They were in the books he read and the movies he watched. The fact that they had been to one made him quiet and thoughtful. Lloyd was glad when they finished their tea. Soon there wouldn't be any more questions about the wallpaper world.

The three would say goodbye and disperse from the Clover Apartments.

Natalia got her guitar where she left it by the door, and Pete turned the handle. He thought they might be looking at the alley again. He was relieved it was only the hallway and the stairs. He pushed the door open and shut and pulled Natalia. He never saw that look on her face before. Worn carpeting led to the elevator. He pressed the button. The car was already there. Maybe it never had time to leave the fifth floor. Maybe they just got off and turned around. Did their adventure really happen? The elevator was cramped, slow, the metal walls were old, painted with a dripping roller. Like one of those old operators in a uniform, Pete stared at the number plate waiting for the dark first-floor number to glow. "Come on."

Natalia watched the narrow gap between the shut elevator door and frame. She could see floors slide by. Five, Four, Three…

Pete said, "Almost there."

"It better not be the wallpaper world."

"I was thinking that too."

The motion stopped. Gears and chains relaxed.

"Here we are." She took his hand.

Lloyd couldn't believe his fortune. He had a safe full of dandelions. This dreamworld wasn't going anywhere for a long while. Thanks to Natalia and Pete. Lloyd was never able to find anyone as good as them. The most he ever got was a few flowers and stems, nobody ever made it to the field. That was like Treasure Island. He got his coat from thin air and put it on and followed them.

14
ANOTHER SATURDAY

There's a block in the York neighborhood that runs along Sunnyside. Cars rush by apartments, a few old houses with porches mumble at the traffic. You can hear them from the sidewalk. The triangle-shaped café on the corner where two streets meet at a traffic light has its name painted on the window: A Terrible Place For A Store. That's not a lie. There's nowhere to park, the only way to it is by foot or parachute. An imaginary subway stop. And yet it's popular enough, especially with younger people who don't have cars, they walk here and go in for coffee and music and talk. The glass on the door and the telephone pole outside are papered with colorful flyers. Natalia's name is on one of them. Tuesday night at 8PM. Her guitar case leans against her knee where she and Pete are sitting at a table in the window with the city driving by.

Pete emptied his cup of water and stood. This was his third trip to the pitcher. That tea Lloyd gave them left their mouths dry. Strange how it seemed to fill them with sand. They figured it must be the heat of the day they were walking in. This café was their oasis. When he got back to their table with their cups, Natalia was playing her guitar.

Pete sat down and listened and while he did, words came to him. A sentence. Then another one. They landed on a scrap of paper he got from his pocket. Then he wrote more. When he set the pen down, he asked her, "What's that song?"

"I don't know its name."

Pete underlined a lyric, "Your favorite dream." He set the paper on her side of the table so she could read it and see if it fit the song. Who knows how these things work. It's possible they come from another world, relayed on invisible wires that stretch for miles. Their song arrived on radio waves. Sometimes, like this time, it came so easy it was like dipping water from a creek they both had a hand in.

Lloyd was glad all they had was a song. A souvenir. There should be nothing more. He stood outside against the wall where he couldn't be seen with an open stopwatch. When you know you're in a dream you can do most anything. A little movie of Pete and Natalia played in a clamshell. Their song was playing softly. The tea shouldn't take long to work. Only Lloyd could see a cloud around them as they found the song and by the time it was done, when the air cleared like cigarette smoke, their memory of the wallpaper world was gone. They didn't know where their song came from.

But Lloyd knew. And a few days away, he returned. He applauded on Tuesday night sitting with a little audience gathered in chairs that were pushed around her. She bowed and said goodnight and have good dreams everyone. A funny thing to say, Lloyd thought.

The stopwatch told Lloyd they were getting ready to leave. The tea had done its job, it was another Saturday, a sunny day with a little forgotten patch of time cut free. Natalia and Pete had a new memory. They left A Terrible Place For A Store and talked and laughed and walking stitched them to the next café. They were excited about "Your Favorite Dream," the way it found them like a cat waking up and rubbing your leg.

Lloyd stood by the telephone pole as they came outside. They looked at him and looked away. He was happy he was someone they had never seen before.

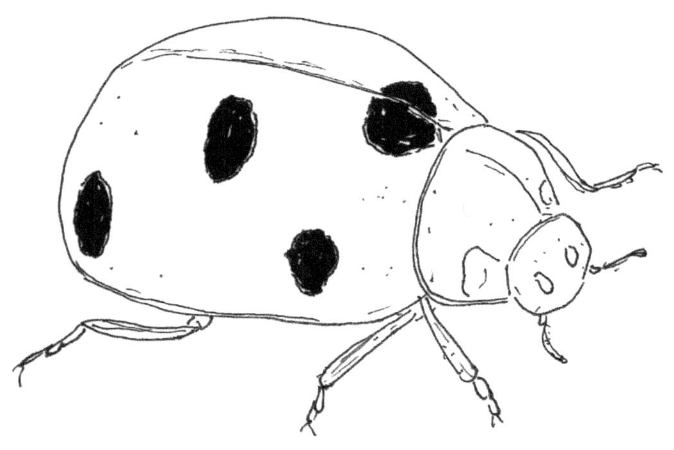

across the ocean

15
YOUR FAVORITE DREAM

DuCanne Recording Studio pressed fifty copies of "Your Favorite Dream." Natalia and Pete carried them to coffeehouses—in those days there were a lot of them: The Globe, The Black Cat, Crooks, The Green Marilyn, So and So's—jukeboxes and the local radio station. That was fun, they were stars in a small way. Then a sailor took the song with him across the ocean to Japan. DuCanne got an order from Tokyo for 3,000. Imagine how the alleys of Shinjuku echoed with her. Then it was in a movie. A girl sang it to a giant ladybug while its volcano island sparked and flamed and sunk into the sea. That ladybug took to the air and returned the melody to America to drive-ins and theaters that welcomed strange sights, onto midnight TV where old monster movies roam *The Count Misfit Show*, one step away from dreams. From there it flew to someone who couldn't sleep, who worked in advertising. The song was catchy, it stuck with you, it became 26 seconds in a Woolworths' commercial. Natalia was fifteen again on the radio, #12 on the Billboard. The song had a life of its own that tracked around the world and found Natalia when she was 64, when she was flown to Burbank Studios to perform on *The Sylvan Moore Show*.

Just her voice and a guitar on television.

Footsteps went to another room. A kitchen light flicked on and buzzed. A glass of water poured. The refrigerator opened and closed. A sandwich was prepared and put on a plate.

"It was a long time ago. My friend Peter and I wrote songs together."

"I understand you haven't seen Peter since then. Is that true?"

She said, "Yes. I guess we just sort of drifted apart. I hoped he might telephone, but—"

"I tell you what," Sylvan Moore took a quick drag off his cigarette, "We have a surprise for you tonight. Would you like to meet our next guest?"

He turned towards the band, "How 'bout it, Tommy? A little fanfare if you don't mind."

The orchestra responded with the chorus of that well-worn song and the blue stage curtain was pushed aside enough to let an old man get through.

16
THE DANDELION DRIVER

It wasn't as hard as Lloyd thought to find other people like himself. He wasn't the only one with a wallpaper roll. A perfect world wasn't always enough, some left. Some were saints who worked miracles, some like Lloyd just wanted to be somewhere else. Occasionally Lloyd would cross paths with them.

Like the time Lloyd met Sam, a dandelion driver who came to America to meet Jack Benny. Radio waves travel through wallpaper. Sam waited for Sunday evening at 7 o'clock the way people behind the Iron Curtain picked up on jazz and Chuck Berry. One day they might invent radio-proof wallpaper, but that day hasn't arrived. While Sam made the rounds from the fields, he tuned in to 1942. It sounded like a room next door. Humor got them through hard times and wars. As he listened, he started to laugh too. He began seeing things in a new way. When Sam got the chance to try a door—if you knew the right person you could borrow one—he jumped. He promised he would hurry. "I know where Mr. Benny lives, 1002 North Roxbury Drive. I just want to say thanks." It wasn't that easy though, he found out time was the trouble, radio travels slow. He told Lloyd, "I got here too late. He's been dead for forty years." Lloyd could sympathize, the people on this side came and went so quickly. But life went on without them. The birds are still singing in the trees, people still laugh at jokes even without Jack Benny.

Some of Lloyd's fellow travelers were less benign. Before Natalia and Pete, Lloyd had some desperate times trying to get flowers. There's a parking lot a block from Safeway. If it needed theme music to set the mood, a rattlesnake would do. He stepped over the chain that kept cars out. The cement had endured years of weather, cooked and cracked. The lot was empty except for a low Packard parked against the back fence. As Lloyd neared, the window rolled down. The driver wore a fedora and a gray coat. Smoke weaved from a cigarette. It was night and the only light came from the green dials on the dashboard and the orange ember when the driver smoked.

"Clatter," the driver said. "What do you know?"

"Well, Delson…" Lloyd stopped next to the car. "I'm looking for some flowers."

"I thought you might be." Delson slipped his hand into his coat and he removed a clear baggie. He got the reaction he wanted. "Four dreams."

"What?"

Delson shrugged. "Price went up."

The bag glowed with a weak yellow light. It wasn't pure that's for sure, it could have been cut with sunlight and stalks, but at the moment it was as close as Lloyd got.

"Speaking of price..." Delson waved a square of paper. The bold letters on it read Wanted and the picture was no stranger. "You got a price on your head, Clatter. I'm impressed. You know I wouldn't sell you out, but there are people that would. That's a pretty decent reward." A roll of wallpaper leaned on the seat. All he needed to do was pull Lloyd through.

This was a world where night took over. A

parking lot and crime.
        Lloyd paid in dreams he stole from sleepers.

69

17
SLEEPERS

Up on a roof in a light winter rain, Lloyd examined the dream machine. It was pulled down hand over hand with its tethered balloon. He opened the lid. There were some good ones. Dreams were like fish in a net, caught in the lining, wriggling against his reach. Picking out the ones he wanted, transferring them to vials, he released the others to drift free. They were too small or torn or dull or old and frayed, nothing Delson would be interested in.

He watched them go. They swam from the building ledge into the air. They would look for their sleepers again to see if they could get back in. If they couldn't make it back, they would fall from the sky. Sometimes Lloyd saw them on windowsills, in cobwebs, sometimes they died on the sidewalks, dry as cellophane. Well, at least he gave them a chance.

Lloyd tied the balloon with its empty chamber to a TV aerial. Then he made it disappear. There was no point letting someone stumble upon it. They wouldn't know what it was, it was far beyond explaining. When he looked at the town again there was no sign of the chaff, not a glimmer of the dreams he let go. A milk truck mumbled as it rounded a corner below, the first robin, and distant chimes coming from a temple bell where the saints woke up early.

Lloyd yawned. He would go downstairs in a minute to his room. Dawn was on the way. He could sleep, but it was still a new thing for him and dreaming wasn't something he was good at yet. If one of his dreams was found captured in his flying machine it wouldn't be worth more than a penny on the street. When you're trading dreams for wallpaper world flowers, they better be good.

His shoulders and the back of his coat were dotted with rain. His coat pocket clinked with little filled vials. The sleepers would wake for work or school. They wouldn't remember their dreams in the morning, they wouldn't be missed, but Lloyd didn't like this business. Meeting Delson in a dark parking lot with his film noir car and smoke was a trap that Lloyd was tangled in.

18
HAVE YOU SEEN LLOYD CLATTER?

Lloyd wanted to think those days were done. He had his dandelion stockpile now, he could lay low. But he was a fugitive, and some who went back and forth between worlds were bounty hunters. He knew they were circling him, but he'd been careless thinking he couldn't be found.

A week had passed since A Terrible Place For A Store. Lloyd was enjoying another spring day or trying to. He didn't go to the cafés where Natalia and Pete might be. That wasn't easy, he missed them. In a few months he would hear her song on the radio. For the rest of his time in America, anytime he heard it, he thought of watching them in his stopwatch when that song was new.

It was lonely on this side of the wallpaper, how could anyone get to know him, what could he say? How could anyone believe he was a dream in their dream? Taylor Avenue was sunny. How far did this dreamworld go? He could make a car, or a helicopter appear, a ship maybe. He wondered about the open sea. For the past few days he'd been walking a mile down Mill Street to the harbor. Get a cup of coffee from a place Natalia and Pete would never be. A few boats were moored in the flat water. He could take one and be gone tonight. If it was going too slow, the boat could transform into a Lockheed Constellation and land him in Japan.

Taylor Avenue stopped at a cliff. The street turned into stairs that ran a hundred feet down the steep overgrown hill to become Taylor again below. The route was like passing through wallpaper, wallpaper made of trees and birds and shadows. If the stairway was water instead of cement, there'd be salmon fighting up the current.

A lamppost awaited Lloyd at the top of the stairs. It's an old steel pillar holding a glowing beehive-shaped lamp. It's seen some wear-and-tear, some dents in the metal, chipping paint, also all the remains of concert posters, teenage bands and Natalia's name. Lloyd's face mirrored back at him on a Wanted poster. Have you seen Lloyd Clatter? He tore it down. The sound of it crumpling into a ball.

And another sound from behind him. A match striking and hands cupping the flame to a cigarette. Delson. "Clatter," Delson said. "What do you know?"

Lloyd knew he was in trouble. Or was he? This was a dream. Couldn't he change what's happening, or should he? Who started this thing he was in and kept it going? Could it be his own doing?

"Turns out I couldn't refuse that reward, Clatter. I let these trackers know where you are." A wallpaper door was wrapped around the trunk of the nearest tree. It flapped open.

"Oh no," said Lloyd. Then he recognized them, and felt a little better.

They were on TV on Saturday mornings. The trackers were Abbott and Costello. Two clowns. This is who they sent to capture him! Suddenly Lloyd realized he had a chance. They weren't in the wallpaper world now, if Lloyd started to run, they were bound by comedy to trip on the stairs or step on roller-skates. And Delson was no threat, he couldn't get far on all those cigarettes. Lloyd judged his distance to the stairway. One, two, three…

19
GOOD CHASE

Lloyd was surprised. They put up a pretty good chase. Also, running in a dream could be challenging, like wading against the undertow. The stairs ended, he jumped on a motorcycle—he didn't know what he was doing exactly, he never rode one before, and it didn't matter—he twisted the right handle grip, and he was speeding down Taylor. He forgot his pursuers could do that too, this was their dream too, they could follow his every move.

Lloyd could become a crow, but that wasn't fast enough, and they would know it was him. He could send himself onto the padded seat of a high-flying Pan Am jet—it wouldn't matter, they would be there too. Abbott and Costello's motorcycle roared alongside and Lou stood up in the sidecar, holding a net big enough to toss over a lion. Lloyd put a gorilla in it and the motorcycle fell behind. In case that wasn't enough, Lloyd added a truck spilling watermelons on the road.

Without even trying, Lloyd was downtown. No motorcycle, no rocket, no antelope chariot. It was hard to know what people in the dream thought of him. He didn't want to draw attention and end up on another Wanted sign: *Lloyd Clatter. Motorcycle Thief and Disturber of the Peace.* He wasn't sure where he was walking to, what he wanted was somewhere to hide for a while. Either his imagination created that place, or it had been here on York Street all along and he just never noticed it before. People in his dream created this world. They set the stage, he was just visiting until he ran out of flowers and woke up. The store was big as Safeway. Tall neon letters stood above the flat roof:

Wallpaper World.

Lloyd didn't look behind himself, that would probably make Bud and Lou and Delson appear. The doors hissed open and he hurried inside.

It really could have been a Safeway: there were tall shelving rows running aisles towards the back wall, yellowy florescent lights, a shiny linoleum floor, a teenager pushing a broom, cashiers in blue aprons, shoppers pushing shopping carts, music in hidden speakers.

"Can I help you find something, sir?"

"No," said Lloyd. He headed down Aisle 4. Rolls of wallpaper standing on end, tall as telephone poles. You could find any color and pattern. Was wallpaper really popular enough to fill a grocery store? Apparently. At the end of the row, he turned the corner and Aisle 5 took him by surprise. Wallpaper doors waited on hangers for a hundred feet. What a selection! He knew he didn't have time to be choosy. He grabbed the soft, blue-colored corner of one, slid it open and hid behind.

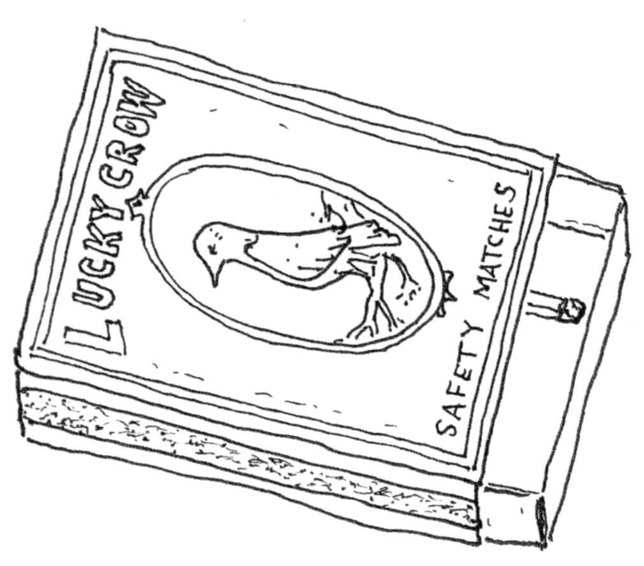

some little spark

20
EVERYDAY WONDERS

There was always the possibility Natalia and Pete might think of the wallpaper world. Some little spark could remind them.

The winters are cold, the gray lasts for months. The rain comes and goes as it pleases. Pete walked to work every morning on the same path he'd worn for years. When the first dandelions appeared in the long grass he couldn't believe it. The bright yellow was electric. He remembered a story Natalia told about her dad feeding crows. Funny, Pete did that now. Maybe it was because of her. Anyway, he carried on the tradition. He tossed a breadcrust and a crow soared in from a branch. The dandelion field was surrounded by paving on all sides. It was a vacant lot that by some miracle had been overlooked by all the city's construction and destruction. When the road was shining in the rain it looked like a river. He'd pretend he was flying over it. He walked that way every workday. A half-hour from home. When he crossed Brooklyn Avenue, chances are he was remembering Natalia. Those days that seemed like years were cut to a few diamond moments. Pete crossing York Street to his job at Wallpaper World.

Natalia's car was full of things she couldn't live without. Suitcases, bags of clothes, mementoes, boxes of books and records, a box of cooking pans that rattled like cymbals. She was moving to another city. A map made a quilt on the seat next to her. An empty coffee cup. Around halfway there, the car ran out of gas and she coasted to the side of the highway. Woods lined the road. She remembered a blue and orange Gull gas station she passed a mile ago. She left a note on the dashboard, I'll be right back, and she locked the doors. Down a scree on the shoulder, the ground was soft and mossy. There were ferns in the brush and tiny white and purple flowers. The sound of the road was fading. Her guitar rode on her back. She imagined deer made this path. Before cars, these were your roads connected to others spread across America. The trees stood aside, the path took her ducking, into another world's postcard clearing full of dandelions.

Everyday wonders came to them. Things happen that seem like premonitions. At night there was always a possibility that dreams might take them to glimpse the wallpaper world before the memory gradually wore away in the day.

on the window

21
AISLE 5

WALLPAPER WORLD
presents
THE BELATERS
Friday 7PM

You couldn't miss the poster, bright yellow paper taped on the window. Pete unlocked the door and locked it behind him. This was early Wednesday morning, the show was in two days. The store kept a folded stage along the back wall behind a layer of wallpaper. Speakers, amps, microphones in a storage closet. It was also where they kept a printing press. There aren't coffee shops like there used to be, but once a month, Pete made sure you could come here and buy a coffee for a dollar and hear a prepared piano, a ukulele song about a giraffe in a neighbor's yard, an author reading from a polka-dot book, then The Belaters. It was ten minutes to eight.

The store was still closed, he had to turn on lights. Pete walked down Aisle 5 on the way to the breakroom to put his sandwich in the fridge and he saw wet shoeprints.

They came from the wallpaper hangings, walking right out of them seemingly.

"Oh great." Pete stopped where they started. The floor was soaked. It took a little nerve to push the other wallpapers aside. They were hanging like doors. There were five of them, nobody was hiding between them. Still, somebody had spilled out with a lot of water.

The footsteps made a trail down the aisle towards the breakroom.

What was he going to do? Call the police? Tell them the place was haunted by a mermaid?

He followed the feet to the back of the store where it was darkest. Great, he thought, then reminded himself yes, it was unnerving to imagine the Creature from the Black Lagoon, but it didn't have to be that. The water led right into the door.

Employees Only. Pete turned the handle and pushed.

Part of him expected the scene from a drive-in movie screen. A giant lobster would clobber him. Pete crept. The room was quiet. Two windows broadcast quiet silver morning light. The footstep puddles were easy to follow, like someone running with a spilling goldfish bowl. They marched past a couple of tables. Pete set his lunch bag down. The footsteps kept going to the door outside.

The handle was wet. Pete stared at his hand, put it back and opened the door.

22
AN ORDINARY WEDNESDAY

The parking lot behind the store wasn't empty. That wasn't uncommon. A car or two was often there if it fell asleep overnight and forgot to go home. The footprints weren't headed to either one though. Pete caught a second's glimpse of a man carrying a wallpaper roll around the fence corner. "Hey!" Pete yelled. The man started to run. Why'd I do that? So much for sneaking up on them. At least it wasn't a giant lobster.

Pete got to the fence, where the corner post bent from bangs and scratches of the trucks that rolled in and out with wallpaper supplies. Two cars went past on Flora Street. Pete saw the man keeping ahead of him. What kind of crazy shoes was he wearing that leaked like the Pacific Ocean?

Pete kept a trotting pace, but the man stayed ahead of him without really seeming to try. His raincoat flapped. Was he standing still, was he sliding along? Those shoes were like waterwheel roller-skates. The thief twisted the stolen wallpaper roll like a canoe paddle and turned onto Aurora Avenue.

Aurora was busy at nearly 8 AM. Cars were in a hurry to get to timeclocks and jobs that lasted all day. Pete was too, so what was he doing chasing a Neptune apparition? Could one roll of wallpaper make that much of a difference? Not one from Aisle 5. It wasn't their premium stock, those were locked in a backroom. Aisle 5 was for hiding cracked walls of old apartment rooms and rental houses that creaked in the wind.

"Hey!" Pete yelled one last time. His throat was raw. He was tired, he wasn't getting any closer. Small as a doll, the tireless thief turned and waved. In the instant it took to blink, a trolley appeared out of nowhere, stopped and let him on and the thief was gone.

"Hey what?"

That voice startled Pete, he didn't know someone was there, on the other side of the telephone pole. Pete was glad it was someone he knew, not some watery villain sneaking up on him. "Slam! Did you see that guy?"

"Who?"

"The one who left all the water footprints."

"Water what?"

"The—" Pete didn't see them anymore. The sidewalk was an ordinary Wednesday. "They're not there." He was chasing a phantom. Slam was real though, already hitting the morning streets with his shoulder bag full of flyers and posters. A stapler in his hand, tape if he needed it, tools of the trade. It was obvious, but Pete asked him, "What are you doing?"

Slam had one boot in the street, leaned back, his black leather sleeves folded like crow wings. He stared at his paper-covered telephone pole thoughtfully, "Just admiring my work!"

"Is that our poster?" The yellow one ten feet off the ground.

"Yeah," Slam laughed. "I put that one up high for the birds to see."

23
BLUE CATALINA

Pete opened the store a little later than usual. That was okay, not many people rushed to a wallpaper store this early, just him and the morning shift. Aisle 5 was fine, no footsteps to be mopped up, it was just missing a roll of Blue Catalina. That color didn't get much attention, it had been there for years, it was a wonder they kept it at all. Living in blue isn't everyone's cup of tea.

Staring at the vacant spot, Pete wondered, why *had* they kept it for so long? He couldn't explain the attraction. And now that it was gone, he felt—

"Hi Pete," Sandra said. She steered a push broom around him and froze. "You sold Blue Catalina!"

"Oh," he said, "Yes."

"This is big news!" She pictured the next front page of *The Wallpaper World News*. A special edition, devoted to this miracle. She held the end of the broom towards him like a microphone, "How on earth did you manage that?"

What could he say? Not the truth. As much as she would love hearing about the store manager chasing a wallpaper thief made of water, splashing in footprints over to Aurora where the man vanished into a Houdini streetcar, would anyone believe it? Did Pete? Except for the missing wallpaper, there was no evidence that the misadventure happened. He could make up anything.

Pete almost told the truth. He told her when he entered the store it was dark except for the morning light from the windows. Quiet. Nothing unusual. He was always the first to arrive. Or so he thought. A sound came from Aisle 5. A luff, like the wind when it catches a sheet on the laundry line. Was Pete scared? No, there was no time for that, he was just doing his job as operations manager. He went to investigate. Past Aisle, 2, 3, 4. An empty metal frame swung down Aisle 5. That's when he saw a ghost. It clutched the Blue Catalina and looked at Pete with eyes he would never forget. "It's okay," Pete said, "You can have it." The ghost floated like a handkerchief. It was gauzy in the dim light, kiting a foot off the floor pulled the rest of the way down the aisle to the wall where it stopped and popped like a balloon, taking Blue Catalina with it.

To be honest, Pete could tell her the truth and outlandish as it sounded, it was the same sort of tabloid sensation that would be right at home in their newspaper. Sandra was pleased. She leaned her broom aside and took notes. She loved it. This was their first ghost story in weeks.

Unless you count Elvis. There was a fine line between believable and fiction in *The Wallpaper World News*. The current issue sat in the rack near the checkout lines. What a story. A blurry photo, the King of Rock n Roll as we remember him in 1954. Elvis Presley time-traveled to the store to buy wallpaper for his mother's house in Tupelo. Below the newspapers you could buy gum and lifesavers.

24
GREEN HEBRIDES

The next front page was a photo of Pete taken ten years ago, standing in Aisle 5 with Blue Catalina. It looked like a flying carpet. It was strange that he chose that wallpaper as a backdrop. It was strange that he never pulled it when they did inventory, when other non-sellers were pruned to make room for new stock. The staff at Wallpaper World guessed Pete was sentimental, they even joked about it, maybe he was married to it. Sandra liked that angle. Pete didn't know what someone looking on might have already guessed. It covered a memory Pete didn't know he carried.

"Excuse me, Mr. Chan."

Pete turned.

A shopper held the current newspaper, told

him how much she liked the story, she'd been a reader for ages, and asked him to sign her copy.

"Sure," he said. He was a celebrity.

"Were you scared?" she asked.

"No. I didn't have time to be, I just watched it happen like a movie." He handed her his autograph and put his pen back in his apron.

"Are there other ghosts around here."

Pete shook his head and smiled, "I don't think so. That's the only one I know about." Wouldn't that be something if there were more, if a ghost came with every roll of wallpaper. A roll of Green Hebrides would include a little old man holding on who would tilt against the wall when you got home. He would stand there all day. At night he might drift off for a while, but he'd be back there in the morning watching you like a cat. Pete thanked his admirer and wished her well.

Anytime he found himself in Aisle 5 he thought of what wasn't there. Blue Catalina. Carried away like a river. An old song came on the intercom and he remembered Natalia. Once she sang that song in the park, by the fish ladder. The winter current tumbled over the rocks. Pete leaned on the railing and watched the salmon submarines returning to the creek from a year at sea.

Funny she would sing a radio song anywhere, she had joie de vivre, like a robin that didn't mind telling the neighborhood when it was spring. He hoped she was still like that.

25
NAYDALENE'S MACHINE

Many many moons after they lost touch, Pete looked for a shop on Aurora Avenue. One of the cashiers told him about the place. Little stores crowded together, clothes racks spilled onto the sidewalk, grills smoked with lunchtime meals. He knew where he was going. It wasn't a Paris landmark, but a weatherbeaten reflection, a conical radio tower rusting up fifty feet from the roof. In the window below, a neon sign sizzled. It spelled Lost and Found. Pete went inside.

An old man in a blue guard's uniform sat in a chair near the door. He might have started standing in a bank or jewelry store, but this is where he ran aground. He gave Pete a sallow look but made no effort to interfere. Pete walked around him. The room didn't have much to guard, three similar machines resembling pinball games moored along a wall. A woman at the counter raised her hand and waved, "Hi."

"Hello," Pete said. He couldn't quite hide his reaction. Her skin was mossy green and she wore a long black robe and a matching pointed hat. "I was hoping…I'd like to find…"

"Person, place, or thing?" she asked.

"Umm, person."

"Okay," she flowed around the counter. "I'm Naydalene," she said.

Pete introduced himself too. He was surprised he never noticed her before on the street or in his store, not that this place had any wallpaper. If anything, it could use some. He could help her with that.

She said, "These are our detectors. If you're familiar with sonar, or radar, it's the same principle." The first machine she approached recognized her and flickered with colored bulbs. A radar dish clumsily spun on top. "This is the Find-Someone 5000. These other two are broken. I called for repair but we're still waiting." She touched the glass screen and the dancing lights responded, circling her hand. "What can you tell me about the person you're looking for?"

"She about my age, a year or two less. Her name is Natalia Viola. She's a musician, she plays guitar and sings. You wouldn't believe how talented." As he remembered, Naydalene pushed the little lights around with her fingertips. "We were in school together. Once we got out of school, I never saw her again. That shouldn't have happened, that's when you need a friend. We wandered out of the flock on our own and faced the world alone I guess. I don't know why we drifted apart. It was a long time ago, I took her for granted, I didn't know better. I just want to know that she's okay. I miss her. I'd like to—"

"Okay," said Naydalene. "Found her."

"You did? Where?"

The Find-Someone 5000 produced the answer on a receipt which she offered to Pete. "This is her telephone number."

Like reading a fortune cookie prediction, Pete held the strip of paper close to his eyes and looked at the numbers. Hard to believe they were all he ever needed to hear her voice again. It was more valuable than anything in a dingy store that was 2/3 faulty, with a guard who was sleeping by the door.

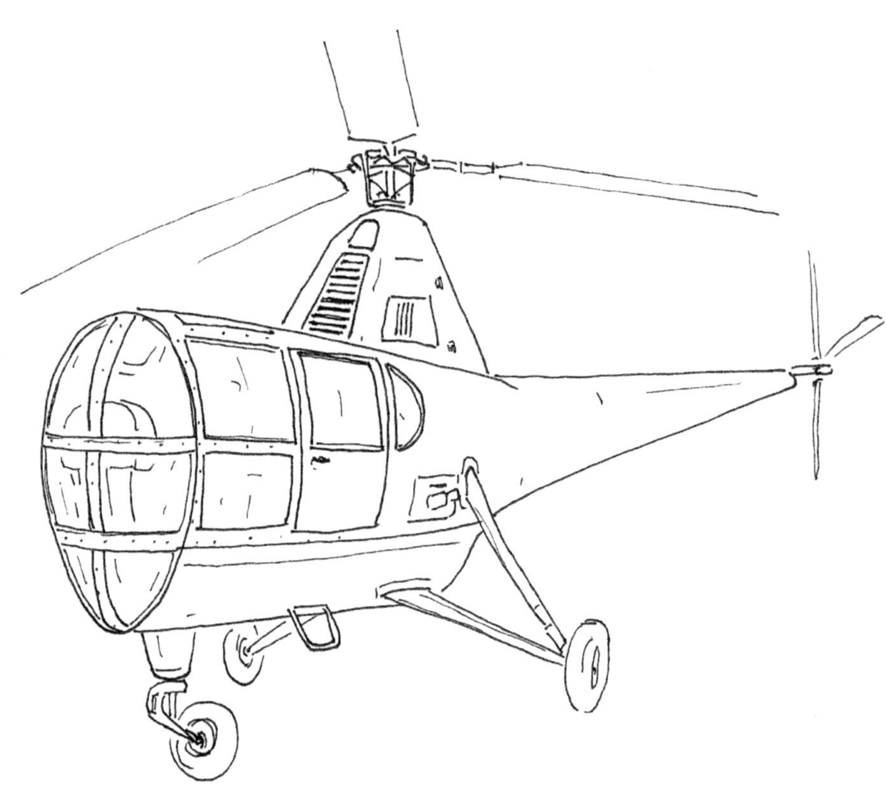

hold it to the sky

26

A MILLION YEARS

Pete used to have her phone number memorized. Calling her when he was fifteen was no big deal, he was calling a friend he saw nearly every day. This was different. He couldn't pretend it was simple as seeing where she wanted to play music today, if she wanted to walk to the thrift store, or look for agates on the beach. They washed up on the shore near the factory steam and clank. You could pick up a yellow pebble, hold it to the sky and see the sun smudging through.

At Wallpaper World he built something he thought she would appreciate. Sure, it was work being there, but he made sure it was more. Starting a newspaper was a fun part of it, and with the talent showcase every month, the next Natalia and

Pete had a chance to appear.

On Flora Street, Pete realized he was walking where those watery footprints had been, and he was holding something just as precious as Blue Catalina. Sandra could have spun a story about another planet that came for that wallpaper roll, that needed that color to cover a hole in their sky. Pete felt that way too as he hurried indoors with his telephone number, heading for the phonebooth at the end of Aisle 8.

Sandra watched him walk past her, as serious as someone who had just seen a ghost. Maybe he had. Maybe that ghost was back, wanting something more than wallpaper this time. She was always on alert for another front page. What if Pete was coming from the parking lot where he was building a magic dome around their store, to keep everyone safe from a ghost invasion? No, she thought, I'll save that one for later, Pete looked like he deserved a rest from the limelight.

A song in the air was interrupted by a crackle and, "Attention shoppers! Don't miss our in-store specials on wallpaper starter kits! Check out the deals on Aisle 1 and stock up today!"

The phonebooth was empty for thirty seconds,

then Pete was inside, closing the glass door. He unscrolled the cigarette-sized paper and pressed it flat on the silver shelf. It made a perfect sail for a walnut boat. A ship bound for wherever her voice would answer. All he had to do was lift the receiver and four quarters dropped into the slot brought the phone to life. He didn't know what he was going to say, he didn't know what she was going to say, each number he dialed was taking him closer to finding out.

The first ring gave him teenage butterflies. They puttered and bounced in him like hail on a car roof. He couldn't believe he was about to hear Natalia for the first time in a million years.

27
CYLINDERS

"Hello?"

Good lord, was that her voice? It couldn't be. A million years had worn her down. Life could do that. Did he expect her to be fifteen forever? He sort of did, she was locked in his memory that way, with her guitar, having coffee, walking beside him under the trees. "Is this Natalia?"

"Who's this? Don?"

"No. This is Pete."

"Pete? Pete who?"

Was she pulling his leg? "Are you Natalia?"

"Nata*leee*," she corrected him.

"Natalie? You're not Natalia? Not Natalia Viola?"

"Naw, it's Voila. Natalie Voila."

"Natalie Voila," he repeated. Half a laugh escaped him. The Find-Someone 5000 was close, but it got it wrong. "Natalie Voila." What a relief! He apologized for calling, she could go back to whatever she was doing in a world he would never know, nor want to know. Her voice could return to the cylinders of a rusting motorcycle. The call ended. The little walnut boat had no wind to fill its sail. At the end of the telephone numbers, where the paper had been torn from the machine were two finely printed words: No Refund.

Don't worry.

It's pretty easy for this writer to tell the future. Most of the time I can see where this story is going. I'm better than the Find-Someone 5000 anyway. Here's one of the things I'm sure of. It isn't over. Pretty soon Natalia Viola will get on a plane. She will be thinking about a lot of things as she looks out the window at the silver wing and the land underneath steadily changing colors. A carpet of yellow canola catches her breath.

This is in the future. A week will pass after the phonebooth failure. Pete stares through the window of Wallpaper World. He watched people come and go in the parking lot. He never expected her to get out of a taxi with her guitar. She shut the door and turned. Pete dropped a can of Woolite Self Cleaning Rug Cleaner. It hit the floor and rolled.

That dream will happen, but not yet.

28
SATORI IN PARIS BAGELS

Pete had one of those days. So much for Lost and Found, goodnight Wallpaper World. He was glad he was walking home. A truck on Brooklyn growled like Natalie Voila gnashing gears, telling him she wasn't Natalia Viola. Pete laughed. Natalia would love that vaudeville routine. If she was walking next to him, she would laugh too. She would be an invisible friend in times like this when something funny had to be shared. She was a ghost, he supposed. One fine day pretty soon, she would be here for real.

The days were getting longer. May was ending. The trees were filling out again. Hard to believe that not so long ago winter made these same streets dark and cold. The seasons were circling round and round.

An old neon sign spelled out Flowers. It didn't need to say that—you could smell them and see them crowding the window. Inside was a tropical cloud. A shop like that set on a mountain top would melt the snow. A city needs flowers to break through the cement. Put in some more vacant lots and you'll see them grow.

A click and click across the street. Slam was stapling a telephone pole. A red and white advertisement. Visit Otto Kott on Aurora for a big carpet sale.

Paris Bagels got Pete's attention. They made a velvety sweet chai that was hard to resist. He couldn't. He opened the door. The narrow room had a long line in the morning, leading past the counter display to the cash register. After five o'clock though, it was getting late, they were starting to close, cleaning and putting away, the accordions on the soundtrack were tired. There weren't many coffee shops like back in the day— here, you got your bagel and coffee and left—no chess players or philosophers or the next Natalia. And a cup for a dollar was gone with the wind. It's fine, that's just time. You can fold it like origami until it's a swan.

He got behind two other people and waited. The racket of a latte being made. Banging and steam like a blacksmith forging horseshoes. Along the wall were landscape paintings for sale. They didn't seem to be made by beatniks in lofts. They rode like windows on a long interstate bus trip. Except for one—it made Pete's heart stop. A view of endless green with dandelions. All of a sudden it occurred—he was there. On the ornamental shelf below, the Buddha woke up and stared at him.

things to read

29
LOTS

The table was scaled with things to read, today's newspaper pulled apart into sections, magazines, a coloring book, a couple paperbacks, a *Wise Penny* shopper's guide, and a magazine about parking lots called *Lots*. That's what she chose to look at. The official publication of the Parking Lot Appreciation Society. Natalia thought that was funny, she didn't know there was such a thing. The cover was a bucolic view of cracked tar, faded painted lines, with a wooden fence in the background. A huge chestnut tree. It was a glorious sight clouding over the lot. The leaves were filled with chestnuts.

She turned the pages. More parking lots. American highways, roads and streets were always running on the go: these were the places where cars came to rest. At grocery stores, plazas, malls, schools, airports, bowling alleys, ballparks, beaches, fields. She never thought much about them. Black and white photos with histories. Stories and testimonies. A photo of Wallpaper World with Pete Chan. Natalia stopped turning pages.

The laundromat around her disappeared, all that mattered was reading this, a ghost story taken from the AP wire service, a one-page glimpse of a parking lot and a friend she once knew. Oh Peter, she thought, what happened to you? There wasn't much to go on, he was manager of a store, which seemed strange when she expected him to have his name on records or books. The story sounded like something he made up, a ghost who steals wallpaper…that's when she remembered there was more. Wallpaper. Was there a door? Did it lead somewhere? A memory was rolled up tight. She pulled at it, but she was afraid. It bumped like a cocoon in the dark.

Wallpaper…Something happened she wasn't meant to know. Is that why she took all the wallpaper out of her house and painted the rooms? Oh Peter, she looked at him. Did he know? In his photograph he was stranded in the middle of tar and cars.

The attendant behind the counter called Natalia three times before she looked up from *Lots*. After all this time she uncovered where she'd been. It was a wonder she wasn't windblown. In Vienna Cleaners clothes are suspended in cloudy bags on the rack. Her best dress was in among them, flying like a heron.

plots that could run

30
SONGS ON THE RADIO

The phone rang. Dark. What time was it? Was it the middle of the night or early morning? Pete sat up. He never slept well anyway. His dreams were tangled out of bargain bins. There were plots that could run in *The Wallpaper World News*. Like Amelia Bedelia getting lost counting sheep, catching forty winks. There were rooms within rooms with the lights turned off. He got out of bed. The phone was still ringing.

Funny, once in a while Pete saw Natalia in a dream. Except that wasn't her, it was her shadow, the voice on the phone was her now.

"Natalia?"

"Hi Peter. How are you?" She laughed. He was

back with her laugh on Brooklyn Avenue after a movie, going to a coffeehouse. She felt the same rush taking her there. "I found you." When he told her he was looking for her too, how he even went to Aurora and asked a robot where she was, and the wrong directions he got, she laughed again. He knew she would. Then she took a breath. "I looked for you too."

"Did you try the Lost and Found?"

"No. I was at a laundromat, believe it or not."

"Did the washing machines tell you where I was?"

"No. I read your story."

"What story?"

"About the ghost of Wallpaper World."

"Oh no, that was made up. It was made up for our newspaper. What really happened was stranger than that. I think you're the only one I can tell." They used to believe each other. They had big dreams. It might have been simpler then to talk about how the future would be. Putting songs on the radio would be so easy. It wasn't though. They both got caught in a tide. He still didn't know why. But he was about to find out. Memories can be moved about. They can even be delayed. He told her about Blue Catalina and the stranger who took it away.

"Peter. I know who that was."

31
PANDORA

All this time Pete didn't see the pattern. It took him all his life until he spoke with Natalia again to put the memories together like a hundred-piece puzzle. Look where he was working! Wallpaper World! Why did he choose that store? He started there right out of school. Part of him was haunted by wallpaper and part of him knew to save Blue Catalina. Lloyd's spare door. What a perfect place to hide it: in a wallpaper store. When Natalia told him about the flowers, he remembered them too. Once you follow the thread you start seeing the pattern. Dandelions. There was a dream city. They could fly. Natalia could remember everything after she saw the magazine. She told Pete they stole flowers for Lloyd. And Pete could see Lloyd plain as day.

It was all coming back, but it was Natalia who asked, "Why are we remembering this now?"

A good question. It followed him.

Pete left his room and locked the door. The hallway creaked to the stairway. The handrail wobbled and the old wooden stairs whinnied. Down four floors on his way to the front door, he checked the mailbox. There was a slanting envelope inside that wasn't a bill or Safeway coupons. No stamp on the letter, just Pete's name. Someone got inside Clover Apartments and dropped the envelope in the slot. The handwriting looked like barbed wire.

He thought about calling Natalia. He had her number now. They could open the letter together in case it was from you-know-who. Lloyd stole all that time away from them, brainwashed them and he took Natalia to the other side of America. He was dangerous. Pete remembered the Wanted poster. Thief and General Nuisance. It was true.

Was it worth walking back up all those stairs though? Pete considered. It was a lot of steps. He didn't even have coffee yet. He didn't have time to call her either, he was already late to work. The envelope wasn't sealed, the open flap showed blue paper inside. It could wait. He put it in his coat pocket. He could call her from work.

Clouds pearled over the city, puddles of blue sky here and there. The sidewalk was muddled with cottonwood lambswool.

Pete stopped before he got to Aurora Avenue. Didn't this happen to Pandora too? And the crow who stole the sun. He had to know what was in the letter.

32
THE LETTER

Pete didn't call Natalia right away. He had to turn on lights and make the rounds of the store before it was open. Nothing out of the ordinary. When he unlocked the doors, he had to put on the manager act. How are you? I'm fine too. Tired, yes, just like you. It's almost Friday though, the end is in sight. Oh, when you get a chance can you restock the pattern samples on Aisle 2? Thanks.

He got caught up in the morning. He didn't get a chance to visit the phonebooth until half past nine.

There was no answer. If only she answered, things would have been different. He hung up. The letter sat on the shelf. He picked it up. What he would have read to her, he recited to the echoey phonebooth instead. Sharp handwriting rowed across a blue page:

Hello Pete,
This is Lloyd. By now you remember me. I'm sure you must be remembering a lot. Time ran out on the amnesia. You've also heard from Natalia. That must be nice. I want to thank you again for the work you two did for me and now that you're both older I want to pay you a substantial sum. It's the least I can do.
I'll see you after work.

Pete remembered how he and Natalia did just what Lloyd said. He didn't like that. Kids will obey though, like school and rules, and there's something a little fearful about adults, as if it's true they created and maintain this illusion. It was an illusion too—Lloyd had shown them that. And then he hid it from them. "I'll see you after work," Pete reread those words and stuffed the letter back into his coat pocket. "You'll see I'm not the same," he added as he opened the phonebooth door.

Wallpaper World was bright and colorful, a song was playing, it was like a fairground Pete thought. He spent years making it a magic place. Like the creek that ran down Aisle 7. Before this was a city, when this land was a forest, the creek was here, with other rivers and streams poured from the hills and springs, water avenues and rain driven streets winding to the sea. Before the store and its parking lot, deer would cross. Imagine all the time the creek was here until cement covered it and tunnels hid it from sight. Pete changed that. He installed a glass floor so anyone can see what lives underneath. Sometimes a kid will lie down on the floor to watch the tiny salmon fry dart back and forth.

Pete wouldn't see the letter again. It stayed in the pocket when he traded his coat for a dream.

33
HAZEL MALTA

Where would Lloyd show up? That was on Pete's mind the rest of the day. He watched customers as 5 o'clock drew near, as the store emptied out, as the parking lot cleared. Someone snuck up on him and said excuse me and Pete jumped. They only wanted to know where Hazel Malta was. "Aisle 3," Pete croaked. "We're closing in two minutes though."

A couple of the cashiers were running their receipts. Pete wasn't going to be careless again. He paced into the next aisle, checking the wallpaper rolls and samples as he went past. He was also watching for water on the floor. Lloyd took Blue Catalina, Pete caught him in the act, maybe a guilty conscience brought him back. Pete stopped at the spot where that wallpaper used to be. He couldn't help checking to see if it had been returned. He didn't expect it to be, but he had to look.

"I couldn't find it."

Pete yelped and spun around.

"Sorry. I didn't mean to scare you."

"That's okay," Pete said. He tried to smile. He looked for a grin amid a smashed china shop and settled for a broken one. The barest glimpse of coffee-stained teeth.

"I can't find the Hazel Malta," she said.

"I'll take you." Pete led the customer to Aisle 4 and turned.

"I thought you said Aisle 3."

Pete said, "Oh. I don't know. It's possible. Maybe I did…I'm ready to go home." A little further and he stopped. The overhead lights blinked off and on. "Closing time. Here it is." There were two rolls.

"Thanks. I'll get this one."

Pete walked with her to the cash registers. Lorna saw them coming and waved them over.

The front doors were locked, no sign of Lloyd. A block of lights was dimmed along the back wall. Normally Pete liked this time of day, when it was over and everyone was going back to another life. Pete returned to his closing rounds. Lorna's machine churned out its receipt. Another ten minutes and Pete would be locking the door on Wallpaper World.

There would be a couple cars left in the big lot, there always were. He would feel like a Wild West sheriff, boot heels cutting into the hard packed dirt of a ghost town's main street. No Lloyd. He would continue to Flora Street, wary as a nightwatchman. Not one who was two years to retirement and spent most of his shift in the breakroom.

As he passed a vacant lot, Pete looked for clues. A suspicious Corolla left to rust in the tall weeds and brush. In the rubble, part of a concrete wall still stood. There was enough space on it to lay a wallpaper door. Maybe it was on the other side. Pete didn't want to check. When Flora ended at Aurora, he would really have to stay on his toes.

34
BLARNEY

A scrap of wallpaper, enough for a dollhouse, door was left on Pete's apartment door. He unpeeled it and read the other side:

I'm up on the roof. Lloyd

If I was smart, I'd leave him there, Pete thought. I'd go inside my room and lock the door. Make a barricade with the table. In spite of himself, he smiled at that thought, picturing everything in his room piled against the door to keep out someone who could walk through wallpaper. He crumpled the note and crammed it in a pocket. At least he could have opened his door and tried calling Natalia. She would tell him not to meet Lloyd alone, wouldn't she? Probably. It made sense.

Instead, Pete followed the worn carpeting to the stairway and climbed to the top. Some of the stairs barked, most of them creaked, some of them bent like trees in the wind. The door to the rooftop waited for him.

The Clover rooftop wasn't one of the highlights of the city, tour buses don't unload pilgrims to clamber up the steps like Blarney Castle, it's just what you'd expect a roof to be, some ducts, a few aerials, three chimneys long since gone cold, a rusted dream machine lying on its side. The view was alright if that's what you were up here for. The sun was headed for sleep beyond the islands. Crows were flying to roosting trees in the park. And Lloyd was sitting on the walled edge of the building, reading a book. He heard Pete and met his eyes.

"Look at you!" Lloyd laughed. "No longer a lad!"

It's Lloyd, Pete thought, but he hasn't changed much, if at all. No wonder—this is his dream—he can be whatever he wants.

Lloyd set his book on the ledge and stood. He began to walk towards Pete—the poor guy was frozen.

Pete saw the book turn into a pigeon and fly off the ledge.

"I wonder how long it's been," Lloyd said. "What year is this? Never mind. It's good to see you again." He was hoping for a handshake, but it didn't seem wise, Pete looked like a sandcastle that could fall apart at the touch. "There sure have been a lot of changes around here. I miss the way the city used to be. I could probably wish it back if I tried." He shrugged. "Do you want to go downstairs? I still have my apartment."

Pete went through the doorway and Lloyd started ahead down the stairs.

"As I told you in my letter, I have a payment for you and Natalia. It wouldn't have been right to give you two such a fortune when you were kids. People would have too many questions."

The noise of their shoes echoed on the wooden waterfall.

35
PUMPKIN BREAD

Three decades of sitting still, Lloyd's apartment was a sleeping curled-up cat. What a long calm nap. There was one difference though, the addition of a new wallpaper door, the Blue Catalina Lloyd stole.

Lloyd said, "It's nice to see the old Clover building again. And you live one floor beneath my old place, how funny is that?"

"Did you make sure I would?" Pete asked. "Was it in my mind all along? You wanted to keep me here?"

Lloyd looked hurt. "How could you think that, Pete? You have free will, you chose where to be, you probably saw a listing in the *Herald* or a sign in the window on the street, right? These are decent apartments and they're cheap. Not that you'll have to worry about that anymore. Tomorrow you could live in luxury on Lemon Island if you want. You can go anywhere, you can do anything, you'll be a millionaire." He grinned, "Isn't that the American dream?"

No, Pete wanted to say, there are other things that are simple and real. If it wasn't for Lloyd's wallpaper world, he felt he could have had them. His life had been turned. He wanted to say that, but Lloyd was doing magic again, opening a cupboard in the air and removing a zippered bag.

Lloyd's grin remained as he presented the gift. "Congratulations. You've just inherited a fortune." And as Pete accepted it, Pete said thanks. It was automatic. It felt like a loaf of pumpkin bread. Lloyd assured him, "Natalia will be getting hers too. Although I must admit she's a little better prepared financially than you. She did alright."

"Did you push us away from each other?"

"No, Pete. You did that."

Pete looked away. He looked at the blue door and the other one, the one he and Natalia went in. He remembered the sound of it crinkling open.

"Ohhh…" Lloyd followed his eyes, "Would

you like to take a look? Just to put your dreams at ease."

"No, I don't think so."

Lloyd laughed, "There's nothing to be afraid of! You remember what it's like there, it's amazing, it's a cartoon world like Dr. Seuss."

Pete was at the wallpaper door. He didn't think he even moved his feet.

"Don't worry, Pete. It's only a window. You're just looking through." Lloyd lifted the wallpaper so they could both see. Pete had a moment where he remembered going in with Natalia. Suddenly Lloyd pushed him into the wallpaper world. Pete fell straightforward and landed on cobblestones.

"I ran out of flowers," said Lloyd. "Get me some. You know where they are."

The door slapped shut and locked. The alley wall where the door had been turned back into bricks, with a Wanted poster reminding citizens to be on the lookout for Lloyd Clatter, Thief and General Nuisance.

36
BUMBLEBEE ENERGY

At first, Pete wondered "Did I go back in time?" He looked at his hands. Maybe you never aged from when you first went into the wallpaper world. Pete was fifteen, he remembered the feeling. He was fifteen and he was happy where he was. Was he though? Faint as a radio signal, he knew he was dreaming. That was okay, that meant he could fly if he wanted to. Flying was like riding an invisible bike. He knew the way to the flowers, he could float off the ground.

He remembered the time he and Natalia were on the bus. They were sitting ahead of a story about bumblebee energy. They looked forward to hearing people like this. You could hear that sort of thing in The Last Exit any day of the week.

A man with a voice like Smiley Burnette was explaining how bees could hover with no effort and that if we could harness that free energy, what a wonderful world it would be. Pete told Natalia that butterflies do the same thing. One landed on his hand last summer and flattened its wings and it levitated.

Where was Natalia? Was she here?

Not in the alley.

Maybe in the busy street ahead. It *was* like a cartoon, one featuring a flying carpet, a trolley wheezing like an accordion, two ostriches pulling a wagon full of yellow flowers—and he remembered, that's right! I'm here to get flowers! Dandelions.

He left his shadow on the cobblestones. He liked dreams where he could fly. It didn't happen that often, he had to remind himself he could do it. Even in his dreams it was a rare ability to remember. If he was able to fly all night, he'd like to spend all his time flying, exploring over oceans and continents.

The field wasn't far. He was flying effortlessly without pedaling, he had that bee energy speeding him over the avenue traffic, down the next alley, past windows, over a wall and the moat monsters below.

Pete was in a dream, a familiar one, and he told himself, change it, look for Natalia. But that command was lost in the hush of landing in tall flowers. Look at them all! They grew to his shoulders. Dandelions wide as saucers. If he was hypnotized, he couldn't break the spell. Lloyd needed these flowers, Pete couldn't leave until he had some. In the sunshine twenty feet overhead, swallows flew spiderweb lines back and forth. There were bees around him. One wore glasses.

When he had a bale of flowers, Pete called for the wallpaper door. Wasn't that how he and Natalia summoned it before? They pictured it—it appeared like a taxi—and Pete tried to hail it again. At first it shimmered like a mirage, a ghost flag, but not for long. The bumblebees circled it. The one with glasses carried a bag full of gold pollen.

all day in a dream

37
KING OF THE CHASE

"Pete calling Lloyd, come in Lloyd…"

The wallpaper fluttered. The door hesitated two feet off the ground. If it would open, Pete could leap over and in. "Pete calling Lloyd… Come in Lloyd." What was taking him? Time was different on the other side—it could seem like all day in a dream while only a minute passed by in the Clover. The wallpaper tensed and started to move.

Imagine you're reading page 137 and when you reach the end, you flip the page. The wallpaper swung aside and Lloyd was looking at ten thousand dandelions. He couldn't hide the look of someone about to lean down and plunge his hands in. It took great restraint not to. If he did, his presence would be felt, he would set off alarms in the wallpaper world.

"Here's your flowers," Pete said. He held them awkwardly, the way he held the carnations he got for Natalia's birthday.

"Quick," Lloyd said, "Throw them in here."

Pete did.

The door shut.

The mirage of wallpaper lasted a moment, then it was gone. Bees flew through the space where it had been.

"Are you Peter Chan?"

This was Pete's day for surprises. He had no radar warning who was on the way. He didn't hear shoes plowing through the tall plants, someone popped into that spot and said his name. When he turned around, he was in for another surprise. It was remarkable. Pete said, "Are you Charlie Chaplin?"

This wasn't the Chaplin from *Modern Times*. He wore a policeman uniform. A cardboard star pinned to the coat. His face was stern, moustache buttoned on, he wasn't looking for laughs. Strange. His black eyes were so serious. What's the point of a world without comedy from the stars? Here in the wallpaper world, he was just like anyone else. "Peter Chan," he said, "You are under arrest."

Maybe Pete could have flown, left Chaplin leaping about helplessly on the ground, but Pete forgot he was in a dream, the wallpaper world was real, he was caught in it. Besides, Pete had often seen Chaplin in the movies, he was King of the Chase. He could scale steep cliffs, flee up escalators, run over roofs, leap through traffic and trolleys, roller-skate, dodge kicks and swings from every sort of person or animal or machine. Pete and Charlie Chaplin shuffled between the rows of flowers. The loam was soft as a pillow. A rowboat was waiting for them in the moat. A silver robot held the oars.

38
CLOUDS IN CLOUDS

Pete still remembered dinosaurs. Fifteen years old wasn't so far from the days he would walk to the library and come home with a stack of picture books. He sat at the back of the boat looking over the edge. The deep water was clear and swimming with names that came to him, "That's a Plesiosaur! There's a couple Ichthyosaurs!"

"Alright, know-it-all, try not to tip the boat, okay?" the robot scolded him.

An Archelon swam underneath them. The library books made dinosaurs look ferocious, these seemed peaceful. Pete could have touched the armored tiles on its shell. A striped fish as long as a picket fence followed. "Where do they come from? They've been extinct for millions of years."

The robot stopped rowing and huffed, "Do you want a tour guide, or someone to row you to the other side?"

"Sorry." Pete was getting a little dizzy anyway, he straightened up and looked ahead.

"Sayyy," the robot stopped rowing again. "I've seen you—you're a thief and general nuisance, aren't you?"

"I didn't want to steal flowers, but I can't return without them."

The robot didn't care. He laughed and started to row, "Yeah, that's you."

Charlie Chaplin sat stone-faced in the bow. He resembled Charlie Chaplin, but the spirit was missing. He could have been another robot on board. If he wasn't in the wallpaper world, if he was a projection on a movie screen, people would be laughing. He would tie a string to his cane and catch a dinosaur.

"This moat seems awful wide," said Pete. "It didn't take this long to fly over."

The oars went back and forth. The robot was in no hurry.

Pete tried to see the other side. "Looks more like an ocean."

The oars were dipping in and out of fog knitting across the waves. The robot answered, "You're lucky I know the way. People get lost out here." The fog quickly covered the water, no more dinosaurs to view, and thickened and boiled over the boat. Pete lost sight of Charlie Chaplin in the clouds. The robot too. There was nothing to see but the ghostly fog. "Listen, you might hear them calling for help."

Pete held his breath. All he heard was creaking and the oars dipping and the faint sigh of the boat gliding. Then he did hear something else—a faint voice—Pete said, "I hear it!"—someone excitedly talking:

"…clock on their side. It's a Seattle lead by five in the fourth quarter…"

"That's my radio," the robot laughed. The oars stopped. The radio faded as he reset his dial. "I got a bet riding on the game. Looks like a close one."

The rowing didn't start again, Pete wondered what the robot was doing, they didn't get tired, did they? Nothing to see. Then he heard a match strike and the fizz as the flame lit a pungent cigar. More clouds in clouds. "You bet on basketball?"

Pete asked.

"We're not supposed to," said the robot. "There's a lot of things you're not supposed to do, that's part of the fun. Like you with those flowers."

"Right. I guess so. But I got caught."

"They've been looking for you for a while. Cheer up. You're not caught yet."

The robot laughed. The fog was unknitting. The air was beginning to clear. Patches of blue sky were showing. Pete could see the robot rowing again. The bow was empty though—Charlie Chaplin was gone.

where the fog was torn

39
HIDE-AND-SEEK

"What happened to him?" Pete looked around the boat. The water showed where the fog was torn. No sign of Charlie Chaplin—if he fell overboard, how long would he last in a moat full of dinosaurs?

The robot ignored that question, "Like I said, you're lucky it's me. I've seen the posters of you and the girl. You're desperados. I like that. I wanted to help you."

"What about Charlie Chaplin?"

"Don't worry about him, he'll be fine, he always is."

Pete guessed that was true.

The fog lifted enough to show they were rowing past a rocky shore. Between a gap in the pine trees, Pete saw the factory smokestacks in the distance making clouds. The water was dark green, seagrass, a patch of yellow seaweed, a seagull cried to another, they were always nearby at the ocean. It reminded Pete of his grandparents' house in a Maine cove leading to the Atlantic, the same light and smell. Blue mussel shells. The same steps that climbed uphill.

"This is the spot," the robot nodded at a sandy beach as wide as a throw rug. He guided the bow over the sand to a stop. "There's a phonebooth up there. Call my brother, he's a taxi driver. He'll take you to a hideout." The robot had a business card. He turned it over and wrote on the back. "This is my number too. Call if you have any more trouble. I'm Wilbur."

Pete took the card. "Thanks, Wilbur. I'm Pete."

The little beach was too familiar, the skipping stones, the rock wall with the notches cut into it, the trees above, the root you could put your foot on for the last step onto the top of the hill. Pete knew this place. He expected to see their house. Summer bees. A bluejay watched him arrive.

Pete was in a forest. Crushed white seashells made a path between the trees, leading to a phonebooth not so far. The windows of it shined. The chickadees darted around. The path crackled as he walked. A red squirrel on a low branch. How am I supposed to get back? he wondered, Did Lloyd strand me? Charlie Chaplin is after me. It's hide-and-seek. I'm a flower thief with a reward for my capture.

Now that he was closer, Pete saw the Wanted poster taped to the glass. This was the start of Pete's life on the run in the wallpaper world and what did he do? He took a pen from his pocket and drew a moustache on his photo. Then he drew one on Natalia. He gave her glasses too.

He entered the booth and took a step towards the telephone.

First, before he called Wilbur's brother, he had to call Natalia. Could you call someone from a dreamed-up world? That didn't occur to him. When he was fifteen, he'd call her all the time. "Guess where I am?" he'd say, a game they liked to play. They liked to call each other from phonebooths. There was one in the Grand Illusion lobby, and The Last Exit had one but when the café was busy it was hard to hear. She called him once from the ferry terminal. Ships and gulls and loudspeakers. Phonebooths were magic rooms where your voice could fly through wires.

147

40
WHAT THEY WANT

Natalia was thinking of Peter when she heard the telephone ring. She knew it would be him when she answered.

"Guess where I am?" he said.

She remembered, "You must be in a phonebooth somewhere, let me think…" She named a few of the places that used to be. Cafés and department stores and booths that stood alone in parks and parking lots.

Until he answered, "I'm stuck in a dream." He told her about going to Lloyd's apartment and how he was tricked into the wallpaper and now he was trapped on the other side. "There's no escape unless someone opens that wallpaper door in Lloyd's room. Can you?"

She held her breath. She was afraid of this happening. Lloyd was back and trouble was too.

"You're the only one who knows where I am."

"I can't, Peter. That's so far away, I have a family here and a job."

"Me too. I'm the operations manager at Wallpaper World. I have to open the store in the morning."

"I'll try, Peter. I'll see what I can do."

"I'm sorry, I know this is hard to believe. If you can't, can you do me a favor at least? I don't know how time works here. Could you call my work in the morning, leave some good excuse about why I'm not there?"

"I—"

"Tell them I got caught in a twister and my balloon crash-landed in Oz."

She laughed. She remembered calling him from the Woolworths. A streamlined telephone booth, underneath the escalator, you could hear the stair machinery and the piano player. Once she requested "Body and Soul" and when it began, she held the phone out the metal door so Peter could hear. They were just kids then, as the saying goes.

His call ended. She called his name a couple

times and shook the receiver like they do in cartoons. It was no use. He's just in a dream. He'll be fine. She didn't like the other thought of him imprisoned in the Clover building, stuck like a fossil behind the wallpaper. She blamed that thought on her son. She watched *Outer Limits* with him every Monday night. This could be one of those stories. She hung up the telephone. He'll be fine. She left the phonebooth and went to work.

Okay, she isn't going to see him, I was wrong. Authors can be wrong. I guess I don't know these characters as well as I thought. They have minds of their own. Once I set them in motion, they do what they want.

41
CANARY YELLOW

Pete thought she hung up on him. He shook the phone like a maraca and listened for her. "Natalia?" It wasn't a million years ago, he couldn't just call her for a bike ride to Green Lake, or to see a movie at the Neptune starting in half an hour.

He didn't feel right about the dead phone.

It was too sudden.

Was she okay?

He should have warned her to watch out for Lloyd. What if Lloyd tricked her into wallpaper too?

Pete still had the business card in his other hand. He'd been absentmindedly thumbing the corner until it was soft.

It was a Bird Taxi business card. Canary yellow, with a black checkered row above and below the words:

Dependable Driver
Call Clanko

Pete dialed the number. While the phone rang, the windows showed night was falling. The booth was next to a dirt lane. In the moonlight it looked like a Raymond Chandler setting. The headlights of a sedan in the trees in a black and white movie.

That was quite a trick—just dial the number and Clanko appears like a genie. Pete left the phonebooth. A quick wave at the driver's shadow. A taxi door opened and Pete headed for it. "Are you Clanko?" he asked before he got in.

"24-7," the robot answered. "Wilbur told me to hide you someplace. You got the Keystone Cops after you, huh?"

Pete hopped on the back seat and shut the door. How was he supposed to answer that?

As the taxi picked up speed, the robot eyes glinted in the rearview mirror. "You look like a college kid. You go to college?"

"No. I'm still in high school."

"You plan on going to college?"

"I don't know. I haven't thought about it."

"You know what Mark Twain said about college?"

"No."

"All schools, all colleges, have two great functions—to confer, and to conceal valuable knowledge." Clanko drummed the steering wheel. The taxi bumped as it swerved off the dirt road onto asphalt. A car horn. "Isn't that a peach?"

"Sure."

"And you know what else he said?"

"No, not memorized."

"I have never let my schooling interfere with my education." Clanko laughed and swung the wheel like a dancing partner. The taxi drifted across two lanes of traffic. More car horns, a flock of geese of them.

Blue lights answered on the road behind them. The wail of a siren.

Pete said, "Did Mark Twain have a quote about police?"

"Oh sure."

Pete said, "I hope it works to get us out of here."

42
CLANKO, CLONKO, AND WILBUR

Officer Clonko peered in the window and growled, "I thought so!"

"Clonko!"

"When you gonna learn how to drive, Clanko?"

"I know, I'm sorry. I got carried away. I was just about to tell my ride what Mark Twain said about the police?"

"That's right," Pete interrupted, "He said they were great. And forgiving. Where would we be without them? Pillars of the city and civilization." When he was really fifteen, Pete would have been terrified to speak like this to police, he never would've dared, but this was the wallpaper world. He had the strange powers of a ghost. Hidden in the back seat shadows.

"I ought to take you down to the station, Clanko. Fingerprint and mugshot you and revoke your license. Send you back to the bumper-car ride at the fair."

"Or put me on a rowboat like Wilbur."

Both robots laughed. That broke the ice. They were brothers again. When Wilbur was little, they used to float him in the pond. The joke was that he never got out of it. Pete listened to them rattle and laugh. Clanko, Clonko, and Wilbur—it sounded like a maritime law office. He thought about leaving the taxi. He wasn't in the dandelion field anymore, maybe he could fly. He was certain he could find a better hideout than Clanko. Sometimes it doesn't feel like you can do much in a dream, it doesn't occur you can do anything, you just move along with the current. The taxi was driving again.

Pete was somewhere new. Just like that.

A boiler room in a basement.

"You'll be plenty safe here," Clanko assured him. He shut the heavy door and latched it on the other side. Pete was alone. A long string attached to a hanging lightbulb waved like a fishing line. The room wasn't that different than a prison cell. No window. Painted bricks. The boiler stood in the middle of the room, hissing, dripping water slowly, steadily into a small round grate in the floor.

Something echoed inside the boiler. Rivets covered it. Could Pete open the hatch and discover it was really a submarine? Would it take him undersea, to the Blue Catalina door? It was no use imagining things. Pete sat with his back against the wall and wondered if he could dream himself into another dream. He tried.

Then he stood. Those three robots sentenced him here. "For my own safety, right?" He tried the door. It was locked. "Thanks."

He wandered along cell walls, looking for a trapdoor or something, until he found a broken piece of brick and he picked it up. He thought of something.

The boiler chuffed at him like a winter radiator.

Pete drew a tall vertical scratch on the wall. He scratched another line at the top, parallel with the floor, then a third line down. It was the best he could do, a chalk door on the wall. He took a step back, sat down and stared at it and wished for Natalia.

43
THE CHAPLIN FILE

Moe Howard brought Zasu Pitts a paper cup of coffee and sat down next to her. "Did you hear about Chaplin?"

"Poor Charlie."

Moe shrugged and took a sip from his coffee cup. He winced. "That's hot!"

A robot approached and Zasu immediately began to type.

"Okay, listen up," the robot said. Zasu's hands flew off the typewriter. She blinked at him. Sergeant Cronco continued, "You've probably heard what happened to Chaplin. He's off the case. We're sending you to work as a team to capture this Pete kid. Be careful. He's crafty. Stay on your toes." Moe and Zasu nodded at him. "And one more thing, we started a fund to buy flowers for Charlie."

"Is he alright?" Zasu asked.

"He'll be fine, he always is." Cronco gave them the Chaplin file. "The boy was last seen following a cab driver into the Clover building."

"I know that place," Zasu said.

"We'll get him, boss," Moe promised.

"I hope you can. This guy's good."

They stared at Cronco trying to convey their competence.

Until Cronco barked, "Okay, that's it, you're on the clock. Get going!" He clapped his metal hands. They fled the table, Moe spilling hot coffee down his sleeve. The office door slammed. After a pause, the handle turned, Zasu snuck back to get the folder she forgot.

Across town at the Evergreen Medical Center, Charlie Chaplin lay in a hospital bed. A tray of untouched food was scooted up close to him. He paid no attention to it. His eyes were staring at Kaye Francis and William Powell in Hawaii on a TV mounted to the wall. The room wasn't quiet, hospital machinery chattered and beeped from the hall. Over his bed, one fluorescent light was left on, buzzing, on the streetside wall the drapes were half drawn. A man in a bee suit shuffled past the window, spraying the hedge.

Charlie coughed. He picked up his napkin and feebly waved it in front of his face.

He stared at the television with glassy eyes.

The hallway door swung open and a robot nurse entered. Her name was printed on a sticker: Clinka. "Mr. Chaplin, you got flowers." She was a little cranky, this was her sixteen-hour day. She took his food tray and put the flowers down. "From your work. There was a card, but I'm not sure where it went."

Chaplin was bandaged up to his neck. His arms in slings. Atop his head sat a black bowler. His eyes followed her carrying the tray away. The door shut, the room was a little quieter, a steamship filled the TV screen. He wished he had been on that instead of a rowboat.

here with you

44
A HAUNTED PLANET

"This is the place," Natalia said. The Clover Apartments rolled past them. She steered the rental car into a space between a Hudson and a station wagon. Her daughter held her ukelele case on her lap. Natalia parked and took a deep breath as she keyed the engine off. "I wish you'd stay in the car, B. I'm scared."

B shook her head, "That's why I'm here with you, mom." [1]

They spent half the day going over the plan, buying tickets and taking a plane. It was too late for second thoughts.

When Natalia joined her daughter on the sidewalk, she smiled at her, "You look like I used

---

1 Author's note: It seems I was wrong about Natalia!

to. I used to carry my guitar everywhere." Down the street was the Clover. The stone had grown darker the way castles do. She took her daughter's free hand. This street felt like a haunted planet.

A man hurried past them. Other people ran from across the street. Something was going on. They were all turning into the alley between Vienna Cleaners and the Clover like bees arriving at a hive.

Natalia and B were drawn into the hum. They couldn't resist the current, anyone who was around felt it too. The alley was crowded. Jostled along the edge of the crowd, they caught glimpses of a zebra and a cart. Surrounded by muttering.

"How'd it get here?"

"Must be from the zoo."

"Or a circus."

Natalia recognized it. She took a step backwards. "Let's go, B." It was the sort of cart they drove in the wallpaper world. Was the wallpaper world leaking in? She thought of her son and *The Twilight Zone*. Were Laurel and Hardy trying to tie up the doorway with rope, tabletops and chairs?

The awning over the sidewalk was gone, CLOVER written on alternating green and white stripes. The memory of it was a postcard old as wisteria.

"You okay?" B asked.

They had to make way for a couple running around them. The zebra would be frontpage news in the *Herald* tomorrow.

The building opened with the same worn brass handle. The same mailboxes along the right-side hall, the same wooden stairway leading up. They made it up three flights when they came to Moe Howard and Zasu Pitts blocking the steps.

Moe showed them a flyer. "Have you seen this mug?"

Peter. Natalia pretended he was someone she'd never seen.

Zasu explained, "We're doing a search of the building." She and her partner turned and continued climbing the steps.

Natalia whispered in B's ear, "We can't let them get to Peter."

"Two floors to go," Moe said as they reached the fourth-floor landing. "Let's pick up the pace."

Natalia said, "I'll stall them. Can you run up there to Lloyd's room and open the wallpaper door?"

B nodded. The stairway squawked under her shoes.

Natalia stepped onto the landing and asked Moe if she could help. While he thought about it, Zasu took her arm, "Of course you can. I can certainly use your help."

45
NATALIA BROOKLYN

With the lights off, her mother used to tell her bedtime stories about an imaginary world. A marble city, the toucan that would follow you when you flew by windows downtown, the animals and trolleys in the street, the creatures that swam the moat, the beautiful dandelion island. She made it seem like a magic place and it was, but now that her daughter was older, she let B know there was more.

There wasn't much to see in the apartment. No furniture, a bare wooden floor. The window let in sunshine. No pictures on the walls, just a wallpaper door. It was real. Lloyd kept his treasure invisible, in a safe in the air she walked right through. B touched the wall and felt the paper edge. It wouldn't be hard to peel. She hoped Peter was still waiting.

He was. He stared at the bricks. At first, he thought it was a bee, but when the sound landed and stopped, the bricks became wallpaper. If Lloyd was back, looking for more flowers, he was out of luck. Pete had nothing. And even if he had flowers, he would sooner put them in the boiler. This building, the Clover or wherever he was, could run on them instead.

Natalia told stories about Peter too. B liked those. She could imagine what their city was like, long days and nights, she could hear it in the music her mother played. The wallpaper world had something to do with it, all falling apart.

The room was so quiet she could hear footsteps climbing the stairs, Moe, Zasu and Natalia making a lot of noise. She quickly fit her fingers under the seam and opened the door.

There he was. Looking at her looking at him.

Was it him though? He should have been as old as Natalia, but he was B's age, the way he was in the stories, the way her mother remembered him, another teenager stuck in a dream.

They stared at each other the way two flowers do.

Pete said, "Natalia?"

"Brooklyn," she said.

Morning
6/23/25

The CAST
in order of appearance

Lloyd Clatter

Natalia Viola

Pete Chan

Laurel & Hardy

John Audubon

Farrell Kramp

Myrtle the Turtle

Sylvan Moore

Sam

Jack Benny

Delson

Abbott & Costello

Slam

Sandra

Elvis Presley

Naydalene

Natalie Voila

The Author

Amelia Bedelia

Dr. Seuss

Smiley Burnett

Charlie Chaplin

Wilbur

Clanko

Mark Twain

Clonko

Moe Howard

Zasu Pitts

Sergeant Cronco

Kay Francis

William Powell

Clinka

Brooklyn Viola

The Wallpaper World

Begun March 25, 2025

Finished June 23, 2025

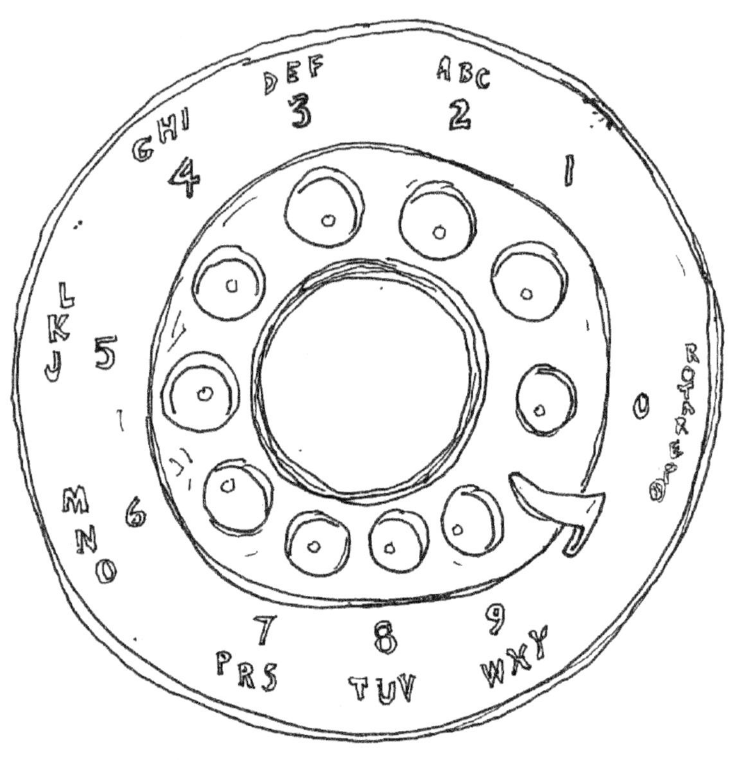

from *The Air Over Paris* (2023)

Books by Good Deed Rain

Saint Lemonade, Allen Frost, 2014. Two novels illustrated by the author in the manner of the old Big Little Books.

Playground, Allen Frost, 2014. Poems collected from seven years of chapbooks.

Roosevelt, Allen Frost, 2015. A Pacific Northwest novel set in July, 1942, when a boy and a girl search for a missing elephant. Illustrated throughout by Fred Sodt.

5 Novels, Allen Frost, 2015. Novels written over five years, featuring circus giants, clockwork animals, detectives and time travelers.

The Sylvan Moore Show, Allen Frost, 2015. A short story omnibus of 193 stories written over 30 years.

Town in a Cloud, Allen Frost, 2015. A three part book of poetry, written during the Bellingham rainy seasons of fall, winter, and spring.

A Flutter of Birds Passing Through Heaven: A Tribute to Robert Sund, 2016. Edited by Allen Frost and Paul Piper. The story of a legendary Ish River poet & artist.

At the Edge of America, Allen Frost, 2016. Two novels in one book blend time travel in a mythical poetic America.

Lake Erie Submarine, Allen Frost, 2016. A two week vacation in Ohio inspired these poems, illustrated by the author.

and Light, Paul Piper, 2016. Poetry written over three years. Illustrated with watercolors by Penny Piper.

The Book of Ticks, Allen Frost, 2017. A giant collection of 8 mysterious adventures featuring Phil Ticks. Illustrated throughout by Aaron Gunderson.

I Can Only Imagine, Allen Frost, 2017. Five adventures of love and heartbreak dreamed in an imaginary world. Cover & color illustrations by Annabelle Barrett.

The Orphanage of Abandoned Teenagers, Allen Frost, 2017. A fictional guide for teens and their parents. Illustrated by the author.

In the Valley of Mystic Light: An Oral History of the Skagit Valley Arts Scene, 2017. A comprehensive illustrated tribute. Edited by Claire Swedberg & Rita Hupy.

Different Planet, Allen Frost, 2017. Four science fiction adventures: reincarnation, robots, talking animals, outer space and clones. Cover & illustrations by Laura Vasyutynska.

Go with the Flow: A Tribute to Clyde Sanborn, 2018. Edited by Allen Frost. The life and art of a timeless river poet. In beautiful living color!

Homeless Sutra, Allen Frost, 2018. Four stories: Sylvan Moore, a flying monk, a water salesman, and a guardian rabbit.

The Lake Walker, Allen Frost 2018. A little novel set in black and white like one of those old European movies about death and life.

A Hundred Dreams Ago, Allen Frost, 2018. A winter book of poetry and prose. Illustrated by Aaron Gunderson.

Almost Animals, Allen Frost, 2018. A collection of linked stories, thinking about what makes us animals.

The Robotic Age, Allen Frost, 2018. A vaudeville magician and his faithful robot track down ghosts. Illustrated throughout by Aaron Gunderson.

Kennedy, Allen Frost, 2018. This sequel to *Roosevelt* is a coming-of-age fable set during two weeks in 1962 in a mythical Kennedyland. Illustrated throughout by Fred Sodt.

Fable, Allen Frost, 2018. There's something going on in this country and I can best relate it in fable: the parable of the rabbits, a bedtime story, and the diary of our trip to Ohio.

Elbows & Knees: Essays & Plays, Allen Frost, 2018. A thrilling collection of writing about some of my favorite subjects, from B-movies to Brautigan.

The Last Paper Stars, Allen Frost 2019. A trip back in time to the 20 year old mind of Frankenstein, and two other worlds of the future.

Walt Amherst is Awake, Allen Frost, 2019. The dreamlife of an office worker. Illustrated throughout by Aaron Gunderson.

When You Smile You Let in Light, Allen Frost, 2019. An atomic love story written by a 23 year old.

Pinocchio in America, Allen Frost, 2019. After 82 years buried underground, Pinocchio returns to life behind a car repair shop in America.

Taking Her Sides on Immortality, Robert Huff, 2019. The long awaited poetry collection from a local, nationally renowned master of words.

Florida, Allen Frost, 2019. Three days in Florida turned into a book of sunshine inspired stories.

Blue Anthem Wailing, Allen Frost, 2019. My first novel written in college is an apocalyptic, Old Testament race through American shadows while Amelia Earhart flies overhead.

The Welfare Office, Allen Frost, 2019. The animals go in and out of the office, leaving these stories as footprints.

Island Air, Allen Frost, 2019. A detective novel featuring haiku, a lost library book and streetsongs.

Imaginary Someone, Allen Frost, 2020. A fictional memoir featuring 45 years of inspirations and obstacles in the life of a writer.

Violet of the Silent Movies, Allen Frost, 2020. A collection of starry-eyed short story poems, illustrated by the author.

The Tin Can Telephone, Allen Frost, 2020. A childhood memory novel set in 1975 Seattle, illustrated by author like a coloring book.

Heaven Crayon, Allen Frost, 2020. How the author's first book *Ohio Trio* would look if printed as a Big Little Book. Illustrated by the author.

Old Salt, Allen Frost, 2020. Authors of a fake novel get chased by tigers. Illustrations by the author.

A Field of Cabbages, Allen Frost, 2020. The sequel to *The Robotic Age* finds our heroes in a race against time to save Sunny Jim's ghost. Illustrated by Aaron Gunderson.

River Road, Allen Frost, 2020. A paperboy delivers the news to a ghost town. Illustrated by the author.

The Puttering Marvel, Allen Frost, 2021. Eleven short stories with illustrations by the author.

Something Bright, Allen Frost, 2021. 106 short story poems walking with you from winter into spring. Illustrated by the author.

The Trillium Witch, Allen Frost, 2021. A detective novel about witches in the Pacific Northwest rain. Illustrated by the author.

Cosmonaut, Allen Frost, 2021. Yuri Gagarin stars in this novel that follows his rocket landing in an American town. Midnight jazz, folk music, mystery and sorcery. Illustrated by the author.

Thriftstore Madonna, Allen Frost, 2021. 124 summer story poems. Illustrated by the author.

Half a Giraffe, Allen Frost, 2021. A magical novel about a counterfeiter and his unusual, beloved pet. Illustrated by the author.

Lexington Brown & The Pond Projector, Allen Frost, 2022. An underwater invention takes three friends through time. Illustrated by Aaron Gunderson.

The Robert Huck Museum, Allen Frost, 2022. The artist's life story told in photographs, woodcuts, paintings, prints and drawings.

Mrs. Magnusson & Friends, Allen Frost, 2022. A collection of 13 stories featuring mystery and magic and ginkgo leaves.

Magic Island, Allen Frost, 2022. There's a memory machine in this magic novel that takes us to college.

A Red Leaf Boat, Allen Frost, 2022. Inspired by Japan, this book of 142 poems is the result of walking in autumn.

Forest & Field, Allen Frost, 2022. 117 forest and field recordings made during the summer months, ending with a lullaby.

The Wires and Circuits of Earth, Allen Frost, 2022. 11 stories from a train station pulp magazine.

The Air Over Paris, Allen Frost, 2023. This novel reveals the truth about semi-sentient speedbumps from Mars.

Neptunalia, Allen Frost, 2023. A movie-novel for Neptune, featuring mystery in a Counterfeit Reality machine. Illustrated by Aaron Gunderson.

The Worrys, Allen Frost, 2023. A family of weasels look for a better life and get it. Illustrated by Tai Vugia.

American Mantra, Allen Frost, 2023. The future needs poetry to sleep at night. Only one man and one woman can save the world. Illustrated by Robert Huck.

One Drop in the Milky Way, Allen Frost, 2023. A novel about retiring, with a little help from a skeleton and Abraham Lincoln.

Follow Your Friend, Allen Frost, 2023. A collection of animals from sewn, stapled, and printed books spanning 34 years of writing.

Holograms from Mars, Allen Frost, 2024. Married Martians try to make do on Earth in this illustrated novel.

The Belateds, Allen Frost, 2024. The Belateds came to Seattle in 1964 and left the four chapters in this novel.

Jones Jr., Allen Frost, 2024. If you're a fan of 1970s television detectives, you'll be at home with this yarn.

Flop, Allen Frost, 2024. The B Minus Gallery presents a timeless work of art, while a seal goes out with the tide and pterodactyls spin in the sky.

Goodwin Plenty, Allen Frost, 2025. An illustrated novel about Mars buying backyards. Let's look in on the Plentys and see what happens.

Do You Know Why You're Here?, Allen Frost, 2025. A strawberry novel, Nostradamus plots, vampires vs. flowers, moonbeam Halloween.

The Wallpaper World, Allen Frost, 2025. Two friends steal flowers from a dream. Ages later, their crime calls them back to the wallpaper door.

Books by Bottom Dog Press

Ohio Trio, Allen Frost, 2001. Three short novels written in magic fields and small towns of Ohio. Reprinted as *Heaven Crayon* in 2020.

Bowl of Water, Allen Frost, 2004. Poetry. From the glass factory to when you wake up.

Another Life, Allen Frost, 2007. Poetry. From the last Ohio morning to the early bird.

Home Recordings, Allen Frost, 2009. Poetry. Dream machinery, filming Caruso, benign time travel.

The Mermaid Translation, Allen Frost, 2010. A bathysphere novel with Philip Marlowe.

Selected Correspondence of Kenneth Patchen, Edited by Larry Smith and Allen Frost, 2012. Amazing artist letters.

The Wonderful Stupid Man, Allen Frost, 2012. Short stories go from Aristotle's first car to the 500 dollar fool.

"The future direction is actually beautiful."

—Yoko Ono